Rainy Days and

Also published by New Guild

The Shield of Mashona
Charlatan
A Child of Silence
Elvis in Wonderland
S.O.S. - Men Against the Sea
Privy to the Mayor's Council
(a two-story anthology)
Melody for Lizzie
Attack and Sink!
The Fourth Service

Dedicated to my better half, for patience and perserverance,
Also to my mother and father,
... and Aggie

Rainy Days and Mondays

Richard Graham

New
GUILD

A New Guild Book

Published by New Era Writer's Guild (UK) Ltd
5 Cogdean Walk, Corfe Mullen
Wimborne Minster, Dorset BH21 3XB

PO Box 11476
Bloubergrant 7443, South Africa
Tel: (+21) 557 6281
Fax (+21) 557 0704

PO Box 100-806
North Shore Mail Centre
Auckland 10, New Zealand
Tel/fax: (+9) 443 8069

Copyright © 1995 New Guild
All rights reserved. No part of this publication may be reproduced, stored in
a retrieval system or transmitted in any form or by any means, electronic,
mechanical, photocopying, recording or otherwise, without the permission
of the copyright holder.

British Library Cataloguing in Publication Data. A catalogue record for
this book is available from the British Libary

ISBN 1 899694 35 8

This book was designed and produced by
Crispin Goodall Design Ltd
463 Ashley Road
Poole, Dorset BH14 OAX

Printed the United Kingdom by Warwick Printing Company Ltd

1

I was halfway down the stairs when I noticed the envelope. White . . . oblong . . . lying innocently enough on the rickety old table in the communal hall. My descent slowed and I approached it with a ridiculous degree of caution.

It was almost ten o'clock, my normal hour for leaving, but by that time the other seven or eight occupants of the flats, most of whom I had only ever heard and very rarely seen, had gone off to fulfil their various roles in society, taking their mail with them. There was never any left.

As I reached the table, I noticed the envelope was addressed to Mr D. Simms. To say I was surprised was putting it mildly. Nobody had ever written to me at the flat, in fact no one knew I lived there. Worse than that, no one cared. I stood mesmerised, almost frightened to touch it. Then slowly it dawned on me: today was my birthday.

Occasionally I'd thought of the people whose birthdays came and went without them ever remembering, and twelve months ago that would never have happened to me. But now one day was very much the same as any other; only Sundays were different. Sundays I didn't work, didn't see anyone, didn't speak to anyone, didn't do anything at all. On Sundays I would just sit in my room and wait for Monday. And this particular Monday, 18 October, 1982, was my birthday. Thirty years old and in a rut, perhaps better put as in a mess, a boring . . . no, a very boring mess, and no sign of a reprieve.

I looked at the mirror in the hall. Like the rest of the place it was pretty grotty, but the reflection wasn't much better. A pale face, the brown hair parted to the right was only slightly receding, but the odd grey hair was starting to show. On a good day I stood around five foot nine but, since the mirror was designed for six-footers, I couldn't see the rest of me. That was actually a shame; the rest of me was about the only thing which seemed to have benefited from my pitiful existence. I'd lost a little weight and was beginning to look quite fit. I put it down to all the walking, brought about by a severe lack of funds.

My attention drifted back to the envelope. The postmark was smudged and I didn't recognise the handwriting, so I did the only natural thing and opened it. Inside was one of those funny, colourful, even rude cards, telling me something about sex on my birthday, but since that didn't apply to me I looked inside to see who'd sent it. A smile stretched across my face – Jim and Sylvia, who else? I didn't realise they knew my address, but it was a nice start to another miserable week.

I put the card back in the envelope, tucked it away in the inside pocket of my jacket and walked out through the front door. The rain had subsided to a steady drizzle; I put up my collar for protection, but it didn't do much good. It's surprising how much water finds its target during a thirty-minute walk.

All the streets and buildings looked the same: tall, grey townhouses glued together, with steps leading up to the front doors, punctuated by the occasional attempt at a recreation area with a few seats and the odd tree. It was the same walk every day. There weren't too many people about, but that was hardly surprising considering the weather. I turned left and walked along a parade of shops, passing under the sign 'Harry Greenaway Turf Accountant'. The door was half open, so I dripped in.

'Don't you possess an umbrella?' the man behind the counter asked.

'I used to . . . a flash one. When you pressed a button on the handle, it went up by itself.'

'What happened to it?'

'Had it nicked.'

We both smiled. 'Thanks for the card,' I said, and meant it.

'I'll confess it was actually Sylvia who remembered . . . but I picked the card.' Jim's tone was one of smug satisfaction.

'I gathered that,' I said, and we both smiled again.

I took off my coat and went through the door in the counter into the office at the back. Jim was on his own.

'Where's 'Arry?' I asked.

'Be in later.'

The office was small. It housed only a table, three telephones, a portable TV set and a sheet showing all the day's races and runners. There were two chairs, but on most days only one would be used; Saturdays and bank holidays were the exception. It was busy then and Jim would sit in the office with Harry to help him settle the bets. On those days, Jim's wife Sylvia would come in to take the wagers over the counter, and Bridget, a young Irish mum, would help her. Bridget's theory was that, since her husband spent most of his Saturdays in the betting shop losing their money, she might as well work there and earn some of it back.

There was a sink at the back of the office; when I say the back, you could actually turn on the taps without getting out of your chair. A kettle stood on the draining board.

'Coffee, Jim?' I shouted through the door.

'Thanks. Look, it's only quarter-to-eleven; what are you doing here? You don't start 'til twelve; why don't you ever have a lie in? It's the same every day.'

'Nothing better to do, I suppose. Anyway, it's warmer here.' Both excuses were the truth.

I made the coffee, instant variety, and resolved that since it was my birthday I'd treat myself to the real thing, plus cream. I'd pick it up on the way home.

I put the two mugs of coffee on the counter just as Harry walked in. He picked up mine and took a mouthful.

'Thanks, David,' he said.

I grinned and made myself another.

Harry Greenaway, 'Arry as he was known to everyone, was a nice guy. He was roughly the same height and build as me, but his hair was grey and thinning and he looked ten years older than he actually was. From some of the things he'd said, Jim and I reckoned he was about fifty-eight. He'd owned the betting shop for the last fifteen years or so; it was his only shop, and I doubted if he made that much out of the business. Contrary to common belief, not all bookies are wealthy. Harry drove an eight-year-old Cortina, lived in a two-bedroom semi and didn't go abroad for his holidays.

The shop itself was small, with only a table and four chairs. It had none of the sophistication of the major bookmaker chains, and some of the clients frequently complained there was nowhere to sit. But, as Harry pointed out, if he moved in any more furniture there'd be no room for the punters.

The clientele was a bit limited; in fact, virtually the same punters put in an appearance every day. They were mostly old age pensioners putting on the ten-pence doubles, trebles and accumulators, hoping to strike it rich. The remainder were the locals who worked in the shops on the parade. They might put on a pound or two simply to break the monotony, add a little excitement to their lives.

That was one of Harry's problems. In his shop, inflation had never really caught up with gambling, nobody ever put enough on to make him rich, and of course even the unluckiest of punters has to win sometimes. Harry's other problems included the weather, when there was no racing for the customers to bet on, but possibly worst of all were the days when all the favourites won. That meant the bookie almost always lost, the OAPs went home happy, and Harry went to the bank to fund his existence. But actually running out of money didn't happen that often, perhaps only once in the two months I'd been there. Still, I doubted if Harry did well, but he always managed to look cheerful . . . old, but cheerful. I liked Harry Greenaway; he'd given me a job, even if it was only looking after Arthur.

I collected the three mugs and rinsed them through. Next came the important job of the day. I sat down in the office and opened the *Sporting Life* to decide which horses to invest my pound on. Really I was no different to the old age punters. I usually put on a 10p Yankee at a total outlay of £1.10p. I couldn't afford any more; often I couldn't even afford that, but it meant I had four horses backed throughout the afternoon, and most days it served to give me an interest, get me through to tea-time. Why I bothered I didn't know; it wasn't as if I had anything to do after tea.

I very rarely won. To do that I needed two winners; that would just about get me my pound back. Three winners would usually show a couple of quid profit, and if all four won, jackpot! Well, dependent upon the starting prices, perhaps £30–£40. Needless to say, I never got four up, but very few people ever do.

Jim came into the office. 'Where's Arthur? He's normally here by now.'

I shrugged my shoulders. 'Don't know, he didn't say anything on Saturday about being late.'

'He's not late, but you know what I mean.'

'Don't panic, he's just come in,' Harry shouted from the counter.

'Still bloody rainin',' Arthur said, as he hung up his coat. 'Sorry I'm late, but had things to do.'

'You're not late,' Jim corrected, 'but we were getting a bit worried.'

Arthur was sixty-eight years old. He lived in a small flat with a wife two years his junior. The flat was about half a mile from the shop and, like me, each day Arthur walked it.

Arthur was the boardman. That meant he worked in the shop on a small raised area to the right of the counter and marked details of winners, prices and betting shows as they were broadcast through the loudspeaker. He was also responsible for writing up the result of each race on the board.

I was the boardman's assistant.

Arthur, although he would never admit it, found it difficult to get the right odds by the right horse and get the results written up correctly. But he was getting on a bit, and on days when there were four or five race meetings, he would often make mistakes or get behind with the results.

It was about two months since I'd walked into the shop and asked for a job. Initially Harry had said there were no vacancies, but then he seemed to reconsider and asked what I wanted to do.

Anything, I'd said, absolutely anything. So Harry explained about Arthur.

He'd worked there for nine years, ever since he'd retired from the railway. Apparently, years ago he'd had some involvement with one of the racing stables up north, but it was never very clear and his stories usually differed each time he told them. Still, everyone liked him, and the punters loved to listen to the tales of his days in the stables. For most of them it was the nearest they'd ever get to the real thing.

Harry was very fond of Arthur; there was no way he would ever have retired him, even if he got to the stage where he couldn't hold the felt-tip pens. The old man had no interest in life except Harry Greenaway Turf Accountant, apart from his wife, of course. She was a lovely lady, always popping into the shop after racing finished just to say hello. It was her way of saying thanks to Harry. She knew the score.

So my job was to keep an eye on Arthur, make sure the results went up quickly and that the shows of betting were recorded correctly. For this mean feat, Harry paid me just about enough to cover my rent and to eat frugally. But I was grateful for anything. I'd just about run out of money when I landed the job. As far as Harry could see, the main problem was going to be Arthur. How would he take to having another employee in the shop? Would he see me as a threat to his job? Harry needn't have worried. Arthur and I got on famously from the beginning.

'Arthur, this is David Simms,' Harry had said. 'I'd like you to look after him, show him the ropes. He's going to be working here for a while; in fact, I think we'll call him your assistant for the first couple of months.'

'Hello, lad,' was all Arthur said, and he continued to call me 'lad' from that moment on. For the first few days he painstakingly explained all the odds and bets. I'd known them backwards for the past four-teen years, but I didn't let on. After I'd been there for almost a week, he took Harry to one side, quietly told him I was coming on well and that he should keep me on.

So, two months later, on my thirtieth birthday, I was standing in a smoky betting shop thinking: Well, I might be broke, I might be mis-erable, but at least I've met three of the nicest people I'm ever likely to meet. What I didn't realise was that there were more to come, but not all quite so nice!

By mid-afternoon I began to think it really was my birthday. A horse called Junction Box had just won the two-thirty, and that gave me three winners from three horses, and at quite reasonable odds. Junction Box's price was six to one; the other two had both come in at three to one. The final horse in my Yankee was due to run in twenty minutes, and the paper estimated its starting price to be even money. Its name was Smoking Penalty and it was very definitely the favourite. Trained by the country's leading trainer, the horse had run twice and won on both occasions. This event was a two-mile flat race, really geared for horses soon to be running over hurdles. The horse's two previous outings were similar races, and both times he'd won quite easily. There were fourteen other runners, none with winning form, and in fact for many of them it was the first time they'd run on a racecourse.

The more I looked at the race, the more confident I became. I made a quick, rough calculation and discovered that, if Smoking Penalty did win, I'd collect almost £60. Even if he lost, I'd still get about £20. But losing was unthinkable . . . it was my birthday after all.

'Er, seen my betting slip, 'Arry?' I asked, somewhat sheepishly.

'Yes, I have . . . you jammy sod. I *was* having quite a good day!' But Harry was smiling. 'It looks as though this last bugger will win as well. Still, I suppose you deserve a bit of luck.'

'What's up?' Jim asked, as I went through to the front.

'I'm about to pick up sixty quid if Smoking Penalty wins.'

'Luck at last, eh? Pity it's gotta be out of 'Arry's coffers.'

'I know, spoils it a bit.'

'Not too much though,' he laughed.

Harry didn't mind his staff betting in the shop as long as he knew exactly what they were doing, but Arthur and I were the only ones who actually took advantage of the perk. Jim had his daily flutter on the way to work with one of the large chains. He always said he didn't believe in taking money off his employer, and then added he didn't believe in taking money off Messrs Ladbroke & Co. either, but since it so rarely happened he wouldn't worry about it.

I told Arthur about my hopes for Smoking Penalty, and got a totally unexpected reaction.

'Oh bloody 'ell, no!' he exclaimed, looking worried and scratching his head.

Arthur was always pleased when I won and consequently I was mystified by his outburst. My face must have shown it.

'No, lad, don't get me wrong,' he said. ''Course I want you to win, it's just that I think Smoking Penalty'll get beat.'

'By what? There's nothing to touch him.'

Arthur, for all his professed knowledge, lost most of the time just like the rest of us, and I briefly wondered if perhaps he was a little jealous. I didn't blame him; he didn't have any money either.

He took my arm and led me to the wall, pointing out the runners in the paper. 'Look, lad, have a couple of quid on this, just to cover yourself.'

He pointed to a horse called Guide. It was having its first run, and for the life of me I couldn't see why he should fancy it. 'Come on, Arthur, this is daft. It's not even shown in the betting.'

But I was wrong. So was the *Sporting Life*. The loudspeaker crackled: *'At Leicester they bet: Ten to eleven number one Smoking Penalty, nine to two number ten Kamru, six to one number four Chee Class, same price number eight Guide.'*

The rest was a haze to me. 'Hells bells, six to one! Somebody must fancy it!' The words were uttered to no one in particular.

'Keep your voice down, lad, and have a few bob on it,' Arthur urged.

I went back to the counter and spoke to Jim. 'Ask 'Arry if I can have a pound on Guide . . . no, make it two.'

'Who?'

'Guide, it's in this race.'

Jim went into the office and was back inside five seconds. 'Yeah, that's okay. Hedging your bets? Think this Guide's got a chance?'

'Well, I don't, but Arthur does; he almost insisted I backed it.'

'Don't worry, yours'll piss it,' Jim said confidently.

The race started two minutes later and, with three furlongs left to run, Smoking Penalty cruised into a four-length lead. The shop was quiet, with everyone listening to the monotone voice of the commentator:

'Past the three-furlong pole, it's Smoking Penalty four to five lengths clear from Pilot Light and Hazy Sunshine, not much between second and third, the rest fairly well bunched two lengths behind.

'Down the home straight and it's still Smoking Penalty by five lengths from Pilot Light. Hazy Sunshine dropping back, Guide making steady headway on the wide outside . . .'

I looked at Jim, Jim looked at me, we both looked at Arthur, who was sitting in one of the chairs, gripping the arms so tightly his knuckles were white.

Many of the nine or ten punters left in the shop were now shouting for their fancied runners, most of them for Smoking Penalty, so I joined in. Despite the noise, the monotone voice could still be heard.

'Coming up with a furlong to run, it's Smoking Penalty by a length and a half from Guide who's still closing, these two clear. Well inside the final furlong, it's Smoking Penalty now being pressed by Guide, nothing between them now. Up to the line and Guide goes on by half a length.'

The familiar groans which emanate from every betting shop at the end of a race contained mine. 'Arthur, where the hell did you find that?'

'Just had a feel for it.' He was still sitting in the chair; I could see small beads of perspiration on his forehead and his hands were trembling. I'd never seen Arthur in such a state before and it worried me a little; something didn't seem right. But perhaps it was just me and the disappointment of not getting my full Yankee.

The final race of the day passed quickly and soon the last of the customers were filing slowly out of the shop, taking with them the same 'if only' stories.

Arthur put on his coat and left. I'd told him I'd do all the sweeping up since he'd given me a winner. Jim was busy cashing up while Harry finished settling the day's bets and I put the rubbish out the back. Then Harry gave me my winnings – just over £30, including Guide. He'd forgotten to deduct the tax, but then he always 'forgot' when Arthur or

I won.

'Doing anything this evening, David?' Jim asked, as he put the money in the safe.

'Oh, same as usual – dinner at the Hilton, then back to the penthouse pad, seduce some little cookie.'

'In that case, Sylvia asked if you'd care to dine at our humble abode. I forgot to ask earlier, so you'd better come . . . I told her I'd let her know if you couldn't make it.'

'Well, put like that, I'd be honoured. The Hilton will still be there tomorrow.'

We left the shop together and started the half-hour stroll to Jim's flat. On the way, he told me he'd won about three quid and asked if I'd mind if we called to pick it up.

The reference to winnings made me think of Arthur. 'With all the excitement of actually winning a few bob, I completely forgot to ask Arthur how much he made this afternoon.'

'Nothing, as far as I'm aware.' Jim sounded as surprised as I was. 'I suppose he could have given his bet straight to 'Arry, but I doubt it. And anyway, 'Arry certainly didn't say anything.'

'You know, Jim, I thought there was something a bit funny this afternoon, but now it's puzzling me even more. If Arthur fancies a horse so strongly he virtually forces me to back it, then why doesn't he? Seems very peculiar.'

We arrived at Ladbrokes and I popped into the supermarket next door for a cheap bottle of wine while Jim went to pick up his winnings. When he emerged from the bookies, he had a kind of vacant expression on his face.

'Guess what?' he said. I made a don't-know type gesture with my hands. 'David, you'll never believe this, but Max who works in there...' he pointed back through Ladbrokes' door, 'said Arthur was in twenty minutes ago and picked up three hundred and fifty quid.'

My mouth fell open but Jim carried on.

'Arthur had fifty pounds to win on Guide.'

'But Arthur hasn't got fifty pounds,' I said seriously.

2

The meal at Jim's was simple but nevertheless enjoyable – most things are when you're used to a diet of beans on toast or bacon sandwiches. Sylvia was a good homely cook, and I liked the steak and kidney pie; I also liked the company. Jim and I drank most of the wine between us; Sylvia jokingly said that if she had more than half a glass Jim might take advantage of her.

The conversation quite naturally centred around Arthur and his remarkable bet. Sylvia, like us, was amazed, not at the amount of money he had won, but at the size of his stake. 'He must have been absolutely certain it was going to win to risk that sort of money,' she said, shaking her head.

'I know,' Jim agreed, 'he can't have much more than fifty quid to his name.'

'Well, he has now,' I threw in, 'and good luck to him.' We all raised our glasses and the room fell silent for a few seconds as we finished what was left of the wine.

Then Sylvia asked the question on everyone's lips. 'But who the devil gave him the tip?'

I shook my head slowly. 'Not anyone from the shop; he'd never have believed them. He's always telling me to take no notice of the punters.' We all agreed it was a mystery, but equally we all agreed we couldn't confront Arthur with our knowledge. He'd be most upset if he thought we'd been spying on him.

At eight-thirty I said my goodbyes and made my way out into the constant drizzle. I wished I knew how to get home by bus, but I didn't have a clue, so I started to walk. I guessed that if I took the route by the betting shop, the way I knew well, it would take me about an hour. If I went the more direct route, which I didn't know, I might save fifteen minutes or so. On the other hand, I might get lost. Being a gambling man and having a reasonable sense of direction, I took the chance.

A quarter of a hour and a good deal of drizzle later, I hadn't got a clue where I was. Not strictly true: I felt I was heading generally in the right direction, but I was becoming less sure every time I turned a corner. I decided it was time to seek advice.

Pedestrians were scarce, so I nipped into the first pub I came to. I thought it only fair to buy a drink before asking for help, so I got myself half a lager and a grumpy barman grudgingly pointed me in the right direction, or so I hoped. From the instructions given, I was pretty sure I wasn't far from Arthur's flat. I didn't know the old man's address but, knowing he liked a drink and that he'd just won a few bob, there was a reasonable chance he'd be out celebrating.

I looked around the room, then put my head into the other bar, but there was no sign of him, so I went back into the street and began to follow the directions for home.

Looking up at the street lights, I could see the rain coming down faster and heavier. I leaned against a lamppost and wished I had a cigarette. It would be stupid to start smoking again, but something was definitely bothering me. I couldn't put my finger on it, but I felt uneasy, like when you're worried about something but don't know what. But I wasn't worried, just uneasy.

Half a mile further along I came to another pub, but again no Arthur. Stupid, I thought, there must be hundreds of hostelries in this neck of the woods; I couldn't check out every one . . . I didn't have enough money.

Five minutes later I walked past one of those nearly all night supermarkets, and it registered: coffee! I'd been promising myself the real thing all day and, since it was unlikely Tesco's would still be open, I went in.

I picked up a packet of pre-packed filter fine, a small carton of cream and tried to fight off the temptation to buy a bottle of whisky. It was a long time since I'd had spirits in the flat, other than those that haunted the place, and even longer since I'd had the money to buy them. I decided that if I moved quickly away from the liquor section the urge would pass, so I made a quick about turn, gave the bottle of Bell's one last lingering look, and caught the leg of my trousers in the racking holding up about a million tins of baked beans. They weren't actually going to fall on me, but I didn't realise that at the time. I flung up both hands in desperation, lost my balance and crashed helplessly into the girl who'd just walked into my aisle. It's funny what things register at times like that. As my head slid off her shoulder and the floor came up to meet me, the only thing I saw clearly was one of those necklaces with a name on it. I rolled over onto my back, looked up at her and said, 'Hello, Katie.'

'How? . . . What?'

Being rugby tackled at nine o'clock on a Monday evening in a supermarket somewhere in SW5 was one thing, but when the lunatic actually knows your name . . . well! She looked understandably terrified.

I struggled to my feet. 'I really am very sorry. I'm not drunk, I promise you, and I read your name on your necklace.' I spoke as reassuringly as I could. I had visions of her screaming 'rape', and me spending the rest of my birthday in one of Her Majesty's guest houses.

She looked as if she didn't know whether to laugh or cry, and I could only stand and stare, willing her to speak. And then she did. 'It was the name that startled me. I really don't know anyone around here, and well . . . hearing my own name, it sort of frightened me. But I'm all right now,' she added.

She must have been about four years younger than me, with short-ish dark hair and a pretty face. Her accent was definitely not London, but I couldn't quite place it. I took to her immediately, and I certainly didn't want her just to walk away, as she was about to.

'Katie . . .' Like a kid anxious for a treat, my voice rose slightly and I fought to control it. 'I know this sounds awfully corny, but today's my birthday and I don't know many people around here either. Would you mind having a quick birthday drink with me?'

She gave one of those disbelieving looks, the sort usually followed by words like 'drop dead' or something similar.

'No, it is . . . honestly,' I said quickly, trying to sound as plausible as possible. It's stupid, but when you're being emphatic about telling the truth, it just sounds as though you're making the whole thing up. She just stood there with an anxious look on her face, until suddenly I became conscious of something sticking in my armpit: it was the birth-day card from Jim in my inside pocket. Jubilantly I whipped it out.

'Look, I can prove it,' I said, fumbling to extract it from the envelope.

She burst out laughing. 'It's okay, I was coming anyway . . . but only for a quick one.'

She was still laughing when we went through the checkout.

'What's the matter now?' I asked.

She giggled even more. 'It's just that you looked like James Bond going for his gun the way you brought out that card.'

I took it as a compliment.

There was a pub just across the road from the supermarket. We went into the lounge bar, which at first glance seemed quite respectable. It wasn't too busy but there were enough people to give it the popular 'local' feel. I guided Katie to a comfortable bench-type seat and asked her what she would like to drink.

'Dry Martini, please.'

I suppose she looked the dry-Martini type.

I went up to the bar and ordered, deciding I'd treat myself to a Scotch and dry. While I waited for the bar person to get the drinks – I say bar person because the gender wasn't quite apparent – I turned to look at my newly found companion. She was fiddling about in her hand-bag, but then she looked up and smiled. I decided that today was definitely going to be a turning point for the better. Funny how wrong you can be.

'Ice and lemon, luv?'

I turned round to see the bar person holding the Martini, with an ice cube poised, ready to drop at my instruction.

'Er, yes please.' I decided more male than female, but I wouldn't have put money on it.

I carried the drinks over and placed them on the table in front of Katie. She raised her glass. 'Happy birthday,' she toasted.

A jukebox stood next to where we were sitting and, since there wasn't any sound coming from it, I leaned over to see what records were on offer. The instructions read: 10p one play, 50p five plays. It always amused me, but I guessed there was some logic to it somewhere. I dropped a 50p piece through the slot and realised the logic was nothing more than a good marketing ploy. I pressed the buttons for the five songs and sat down again.

As the first notes squeezed out through the amplifier, Katie asked if I liked Fleetwood Mac. I was amazed she'd recognised the song so quickly; it wasn't one of their well-known hits.

'It's not so much the artists I like,' I explained, 'as the music itself. I'm afraid I'm absolutely addicted to most music from the mid-sixties through to the late seventies. Living in the past, I guess.'

'But I love that era too. I just can't seem to get into today's music.'

We had something in common already. 'Perhaps we're just getting old,' I teased.

'Well, you certainly are,' she laughed, holding up her glass again. 'After all, it is your birthday.'

For the next twenty minutes or so we talked about our various musical likes and dislikes, and it was amazing just how similar our tastes actually were. I was just telling her about the huge stack of cassettes in my flat, all containing recordings from 'our' era, when I realised something was disturbing her.

'What's the matter?' I asked.

'There's a man at the bar; he keeps staring at us.'

I looked around to see Arthur peering across the room, a pint in his hand. Typical, I thought. I spend half the evening looking for him, then when I find better things to do, he pops up like a bad penny. He gave a wave and I half-heartedly waved back.

'Do you know him?' Katie asked, surprised.

'No, I usually wave at most old men in pubs.'

'Didn't your mother ever tell you about sarcasm?' she said sternly, but the smile in her voice showed through.

Arthur was making his way over. He looked a little unsteady on his feet, and stopped just in front of our table. For one horrific moment I thought he was going to knock it over, so I quickly picked up my glass.

'Arthur, this is Katie,' I said, sounding pretty miserable.

'Pleased to meet you, luv.' He held out his hand, grasping the table with the other.

'Mind if I join you? I'll get my drink.' He didn't wait for a reply, just turned around and staggered back to the bar to retrieve his pint.

'He looks as if he's had a few,' Katie observed, and I had to agree. 'Look,' she continued, 'I'll leave you to him. I did say a quick drink and I really must go.'

'I'll walk you home then.' I thought it worth a try.

'No, you stay and look after your friend. I think he's more in need of walking home than I am.'

I started to object, but unfortunately she insisted. By the time she'd put on her coat, Arthur was staggering back towards us, showering everyone in his path with best bitter.

'Can I see you again?' I asked, saying a mental prayer at the same time.

She looked at me hesitantly.

'Please,' I pressed.

'Well, when?' She sounded unsure.

'Any time... tomorrow?... Say seven-thirty?'

'All right, I'll meet you outside the supermarket.' With that she turned and left. I wondered if I'd ever see her again.

Still, I'd set out to find Arthur, and here he was . . . slumped in the seat just vacated by its previous occupant.

'I didn't know you had a young lady.' Arthur's voice was a little slurred, but not as bad as I'd expected.

'How many have you had?' I asked sternly.

'Young ladies?'

'Drinks, you fool.'

'Oh, only a couple.'

'Celebrating something?'

I got us another drink, and when Arthur wanted to pay I told him it was my treat for my birthday, and because I'd won a few pounds that afternoon, courtesy of his tip.

'There'll be more where that came from,' he grinned.

A twinge of excitement ran through my body. 'That was incredible information, Arthur. Have you got more?'

'Not yet, but I will have.'

'Where are you getting it from? You know what you've always said about tips.'

'Ah, but this is different, lad.' He looked very pleased with himself.

'Come on, Arthur, you can't keep me in suspense like this.'

He obviously wanted to tell, but wasn't sure if he should. 'Look, lad,' he said, as seriously as he could in his inebriated state, 'if I show you it, you mustn't breathe a word about it . . . not to anyone.'

'Show me what?'

He reached into his pocket and produced a piece of paper. It was a neatly typed letter and it explained a lot about the afternoon's events.

17

I read it slowly:

Dear Mr Clifford,

Please forgive my writing to you like this, but I would like to ask for your help in a matter which will certainly be to your advantage. I am a professional gambler with many reliable contacts in the racing world. For the past two years I have been so successful that even the largest bookmakers have closed my accounts, and I now find it virtually impossible to place bets. I have been forced into retirement, although not that I mind because I shall live in luxury for the rest of my days. I would, however, like to take the country's bookmakers for one last 'ride'.

In approximately four weeks' time, a certain horse will win a certain race at quite rewarding odds. I know this for a fact; there is no possibility of the horse losing. As a farewell gesture to my bookmaking friends, I intend to win over half a million pounds, and what's more, I intend to win it using their money as my stake. I have engaged a number of people countrywide to place bets for me, and I would like you to join us for this final coup. I know this letter will come as a surprise, but I have done my homework and chosen my accomplices well. I have chosen you because of your racing background, but also because I know you to be a man of integrity, a man I can trust.

The plan is simple. During the next four weeks I will have information on four or five horses which all have a very good chance of winning at reasonable odds. They are by no means certainties, and don't be surprised if one or two are beaten. However, the winners will ensure sufficient profits for my stake in the coup. I will usually post the name of the horse, together with my stake, to arrive at your home the day before the race or on the actual race day itself. All you need to do is place the bet.

Of course I do not expect you to do this for nothing, therefore you should keep ten per cent of the total winnings plus any loose change for yourself. Should the horse lose, I will enclose an additional £10 note as payment with my next letter.

The plan actually starts today. My initial stake of £50 is enclosed together with a pre-paid envelope in which to return the winnings, in cash. Should you decide not to participate, then return the £50 using the envelope provided and I will not bother you again.

Hopefully you will join me, and the horse to back is:

GUIDE – 3 p.m., Leicester, 18 October

C. A. Davidson

So that's where Arthur got his money from! Well, Mr Davidson certainly seemed to have covered everything. I looked up. 'So who the hell is C. A. Davidson, Arthur?'

'I've no idea . . . never 'eard of him.'

'Then why write to you and send you fifty quid to put on a horse?'

'I don't know and what's more I don't care, as long as he keeps sending tips like Guide. Perhaps it's like he says in the letter; I used to be in racing, maybe he knows me from my days in the stables.'

I doubted it, but like Arthur said, why care? We finished our drinks and I told Arthur I'd walk back home with him. He was a bit the worse for wear and, as I jokingly told him, he was now far too valuable a property to risk being knocked over by a bus.

It was still drizzling as we went outside and walked the short distance to his flat.

'Come in and say hello to the missus, lad,' he insisted as we got near.

We walked through the front door of the block and up to the first floor. After fumbling through his pockets for the key, Arthur eventually knocked on the door, just at the same moment as his wife, who'd obviously heard the commotion, opened it. The net result was Arthur tumbling in like a clown at a circus; fortunately he ended up on the settee which cushioned his landing. I followed him in, but in a much more sedate manner.

'Oh hello, David,' Mrs Clifford greeted, without batting an eyelid. 'Brought him home, I see. Well, sit yourself down and I'll get you a coffee.'

I did as I was told and sat in an armchair opposite the settee where Arthur lay sprawled. Mrs C. attempted to get his coat off – she was obviously quite used to it and I didn't feel I should intervene or offer assistance. She eventually succeeded in her task, propping him as upright as she could get him, before disappearing into the kitchen. She didn't seem to mind that he was quite well oiled, although she did tell him off light-heartedly. They seemed a happy couple; I was almost envious. I hoped that when I was her age I'd be as happy with someone I could care for.

The coffee arrived, instant, and inevitably the conversation returned to the inevitable.

'I suppose he's told you about the letter?' Mrs C's voice sounded disturbed.

'Yes, he has.'

'Seems a bit strange to me . . . a total stranger singling out Arthur to put bets on for him.'

'Well, it is a bit strange,' I agreed, 'but then I suppose everyone who's received this letter is going to feel the same way.'

'I guess you're right. Anyway, he's committed to it now, so I just hope we can make a few bob out of it. We could do with the money.'

'It's like the original gift-horse, isn't it?'

'It is, and I suppose we shouldn't look it in the mouth.'

By this time Arthur was snoring, so I finished my coffee and left quietly.

Outside the rain was falling heavier than before, so I quickened my step in the general direction of home. It had been a most eventful birthday: winning on the horses, meeting Katie, and now the possibility of winning even more money on some stranger's tips.

As I walked through the rain, I reasoned that I should be feeling happier than I had for months, but although my spirits had been lifted something still seemed to be bothering me.

I arrived back at my flat and put the coffee on the table rather than in the cupboard; that way I could smell its aroma rather than the damp.

I perched on the bed while I waited for the kettle to boil and looked soberly at my surroundings. Was this all I had to show for my thirty years?

My 'flat' in reality was no more than a grimy bedsit in the attic of an old house lost somewhere in the depths of Earls Court. And cold! Hell, it was cold.

Reluctantly I got up and switched on the fan heater, feeding the remainder of my 50p pieces into the insatiable meter to coax a small degree of warmth into the room. The trouble was, the heat always seemed in a hurry to leave. I didn't blame it; our only difference was that the heat appeared to have somewhere to go.

I collapsed onto the bed. Like the rest of the room it was old; the wardrobe was old; the two armchairs were old. The only thing that stood out was the cassette player and two speakers, but even they stood on an old shelf. I looked thankfully at the row of cassettes stacked neatly by the speakers. If it hadn't been for the music, I seriously wondered if I would have survived the last few months.

I pulled myself up and selected a Carpenters' tape, and with the press of a button the American's voice filled the room.

I put my old brown jacket back in the wardrobe and looked sadly at the three suits hanging there: dark grey with faint blue stripes, navy for the more formal occasions (that was a laugh!) and beige. All good cloth, all well cut, all expensive and all destined to stay in the wardrobe. I ran my fingers lightly down a sleeve and wondered if I'd ever get to wear them again.

In comparison to Monday, Tuesday was quite boring. I told Jim, with Arthur's permission, about the letter, and we discussed it over a cup of instant coffee in a local café after the day's racing.

Jim said he'd heard of people placing bets for professional gamblers, but he had to agree it was a mystery why Arthur should be chosen. However, we both seemed to adopt the same philosophy: don't knock it, back it. Guide was the proof of the pudding.

I didn't mention my new lady friend to Jim in case she didn't turn up. But at seven-thirty we met as arranged outside the supermarket. I hoped she wasn't expecting to be taken out for dinner because I couldn't afford it, but I offered anyway. Fortunately she'd already eaten and said a drink would be fine. I wasn't going to chance meeting Arthur again, so we walked for about half a mile until we found a decent looking pub.

'I wondered if you'd turn up,' I said honestly, as I put the dry Martini and half a lager on the table.

'I shouldn't have really. I'm not normally picked up in supermarkets, or anywhere else, come to that. But you did seem rather harmless and anyone who likes all those old records can't be too bad.'

We talked until they threw us out at closing time. She had been in London for about a month and worked for a typing agency, moving to a different company almost every week. She said she didn't like it very much, but the money was good. Naturally she asked what I did for a living, but I glossed over it; after all, being a boardman's assistant is hardly impressive. I also glossed over what I was doing working in London by saying, quite truthfully, that I couldn't get a job in my home town in the Midlands.

She originated from Bristol but, since I'd never been there in my life, we didn't pursue it. I really should have done.

Outside the pub, I was just about to say it hadn't rained all day when large spots darkened the pavement. Katie had an umbrella in her handbag, so we took shelter and strolled up the road. I was very tempted to put my arm around her, but I was worried I might frighten her away. Our chat in the pub had been purely platonic and, although we were getting on extremely well, she gave no indication of wanting it to go further.

As we reached the supermarket, I asked her where she lived.

'Just over there.' She pointed through a short alleyway.

'I'll see you to the door.'

'No, don't worry. It's a maze of small streets and I'd worry you'd never find your way back again.'

I said I didn't like the idea of her walking anywhere on her own, but she insisted, and I was beginning to realise that once she'd made up her mind there was no point in trying to change it.

'Would you have dinner at my flat one evening? We could listen to my cassettes and save a fortune on jukeboxes.' It was silly, but I felt almost embarrassed asking, and once again I saw that doubting look appear on her face. 'Just dinner,' I added. She still didn't say anything. 'How about Saturday?' I continued hopefully.

'I can't Saturday. I go home most weekends, otherwise my mum worries.'

We both laughed.

'Monday then?'

'Okay, Monday.' She didn't sound too happy about it, but suddenly there was that smile again. 'I'll look forward to it. Shall we meet here?'

I nodded. 'Yes, that's fine. Say seven-thirty?'

'Goodnight, David.'

'Goodnight, Katie.'

It sounded corny, like something out of *The Waltons*, but I didn't care – I felt like a schoolkid again, so why shouldn't I act like one?

She disappeared down the alley and I started to stroll home. The rain had stopped but the wind had got up, so I hunched my shoulders and walked faster.

The thought of dinner with Katie kept me from noticing the cold too much, but I still had that stupid not-so-sure-what feeling. It was nothing to do with Katie Brown, nor with Arthur Clifford, so I decided to ignore it and pushed it to the back of my mind.

Back at the flat, I put a cassette on and made a pot of fresh coffee. Then I sat down and listened to Rod Stewart and thought just how much I liked Katie.

Nothing much happened until Saturday. It was just after ten in the morning and the shop was fairly quiet; that was until Arthur burst in, acting like a man possessed. He grabbed my arm and dragged me over to the *Sporting Life*, which I'd only just pinned on the wall. His hand was shaking as he pointed to the two o'clock at Huntingdon, and in particular to a horse called Wellington Day.

He produced a piece of paper from his pocket and thrust it into my hand. On it was neatly typed:

Saturday, 23 October, Huntingdon 2 p.m.

Wellington Day – £50 to win

'I've got the fifty quid,' he whispered. 'Could you put it on for me, lad?'

'No problem. I'll have a couple on it myself.'

We told Jim, and together Jim and I read the *Life*'s write-up on the race. It was for four-year-old hurdlers, and the article suggested the runners were a very moderate lot and it wouldn't take much winning. Of Wellington Day it said that he was well bred, that it was his first time over hurdles and that he'd previously run on the flat, but never seemed very keen to race. The best he'd managed was a third in a handicap at Nottingham. It estimated his starting price to be nine to one.

I calculated I could afford a fiver on it, and so did Arthur and Jim. I chose a betting shop where no one would know me and put on the collective £65 to win.

At ten-to-two there were three very tense people in H. Greenaway Turf Accountant. We stood anxiously waiting for the speaker to crackle the odds through the wires. When it suddenly did exude signs of life, I was so nervous I jumped at the sound and dropped my felt-tipped pen. I'd offered to mark the prices myself for this race, let Arthur sit it out since he was in no fit state to do anything.

'*They bet at Huntingdon: three to one number six Droffatts, seven to two number eleven Green Leaves Lane, six to one number eighteen Wellington Day.*'

There it was, six to one! We all three seemed to look knowingly at each other. I put down the other prices without really listening, then a couple of minutes later the speaker crackled again:

'*At Huntingdon, five to two number eighteen Wellington Day, and that's okay.*'

Arthur, Jim and I were amazed. For the price to suddenly drop from six to one to two-and-a-half to one meant someone must have put a great deal of money on the horse. Even the commentator had queried the price before broadcasting it.

Jim beckoned me over to the counter, only to whisper, 'Bloody 'ell!'

'Quite,' was all I could manage.

But it didn't end there. Even while we spoke, Wellington Day dropped to two to one, and then seven to four.

There was no commentary on the race; Huntingdon was the minor meeting and Stratford took precedence, so we had an agonising few minutes' wait for the winner. Just as we thought we could bear the suspense no longer, the commentator interrupted his narration on the Stratford race.

'*The result from Huntingdon . . .*'

We froze.

'*First, number eighteen, Wellington Day.*'

To the amazement of all the elderly punters, Mr Greenaway's three full-time employees cheered; in fact I totally missed the second and third and had to wait for the result to be repeated. In the meantime, Harry put his head around the corner of the office to ask what the hell was going on. Jim, who was supposed to be in with Harry settling bets, told him we'd just had a little win, then went into the back to help out. Being Saturday, Jim's wife, Sylvia, was behind the counter; she gave me a knowing wink.

As the day's racing neared its close, I popped out of the shop and collected our winnings. Arthur took his cut out of our ace-tipster's returns, put the balance in the envelope and sent it off.

By this time the horse-racing had finished and most of the customers had gone home, but there were still a few stragglers staying on for the greyhounds. Arthur admitted he felt tired after the day's excitement and, since he had very little to do, asked Harry if he could go home. Harry obliged.

It was dark outside and looked quite cold. The few remaining gamblers decided the dogs weren't running as they really should and they left too. Jim and Sylvia cashed up and I began to sweep all the crumpled betting slips, cigarette ends and other rubbish into a large black plastic bag. Sylvia offered to help, but I said I wasn't in a hurry, so she and Jim said their goodnights and went out into the weather. I closed the door after them. A number of Chelsea supporters were beginning to file past the shop on their way home from the match and, from the looks on their faces, Chelsea hadn't had a good afternoon.

Harry came out of the office. 'Just you and me, David? Fancy a coffee before we go?'

I said I did and Harry put the kettle on. As he came back out with the two steaming mugs, he told me to lock the front door. 'I've just seen the football results on television. The last thing I want is a load of unhappy supporters coming in here only to find that not only has their team lost, but their horses have too.' Chelsea wasn't renowned for having the most peaceful supporters in the country, so I clicked the latch down on the door.

We were sitting at the table in the punters' part of the shop talking about nothing in particular, when suddenly the front window seemed to explode and we were showered with frosted glass. I leapt out of my chair and, half reflex, half fright, tried to drag Harry behind the counter. He seemed to read my thoughts.

'It's not a bomb,' he said dejectedly, and pointed to the house brick lying on the floor amongst the glass. I dashed to the door, unlocked it and ran outside. There were a few people staring at the wrecked windows, but no sign of the culprit.

'Anybody see who did it?' I shouted hopefully, but the response was typical: they just walked away, not wanting to get involved.

Back inside, Harry was still sitting where I'd left him. He looked up as I walked in. 'Go home, David. I'll clear this up.' He sounded weary.

'Come on, 'Arry, I'm not leaving yet. I might as well clear up here as clear up at home. At least I've got somebody to talk to here.'

In fact, Harry hardly spoke a word. He just looked miserable and got on with clearing the debris. I rang the local police station; Harry said it was hardly worth it, and he was right. A young bobby arrived on the scene just as we were trying to board up the window. He said exactly what we thought: almost certainly unhappy football supporters who'd no love for bookmakers and decided to prove it. There was no chance of catching them.

Having secured the hole where the window had been as best we could,

I told Harry I'd take him for a drink. He declined, until I explained it wasn't an offer, it was an order, and then at last he smiled.

'All right, just one, but first I'll have to put the money in the night safe at the bank. I can't risk leaving it on the premises with the window as it is.'

We went into the office and he unlocked the safe. He took out about £200, obviously not a good day for the book, and put it into the wallet for banking. Then, to my amazement, he peeled back a piece of the wallpaper, removed a brick from the wall, and took out another wad of notes.

'What the hell's that?'

'It's money, you berk. What's it look like?'

'Well, I know it's money, but what's it doing there?'

'It's my reserve fund. I always keep three hundred there just in case, but I can't risk leaving it now. Not even Jim knows about this hiding place, so not a word, David, please.'

I promised to say nothing and we went via the night safe to a pub. Over the drinks Harry, obviously feeling a bit better, took on the role of father figure.

'Isn't it time you got yourself a proper job, David? I mean, you can't keep working for the pittance I pay all your life, and I'd have thought your difficulties would have been over and done with by now.'

'Well, actually, 'Arry, I was hoping that in a few years' time Arthur would retire and you might promote me to boardman.' Harry was not amused, so I quickly changed tack. 'Seriously though, at the moment I'm quite happy with my lot. See this as a period of recuperation if you like. I'll start looking for a job again, probably quite soon.' I hesitated, and then took the plunge. 'I've met a girl, you see, and I don't want to let her go.'

I told Harry about Katie and the more I talked, the more I realised just how much I liked her.

'Did you say she's coming for dinner on Monday night?'

I nodded.

'Well, why don't you borrow my car; at least that way you can drive her home.'

'Oh 'Arry!' I almost shouted. 'Why should I ever want to leave this job when I've got such a super boss as you?'

I spent Sunday wishing for Monday; nothing unusual in that, but this time I had something definite to look forward to. I bought a *Sunday Express* and noticed in the racing results that Wellington Day had won by no less than twenty lengths. I estimated that to be about forty or fifty yards, a nice way to win a race. I raised my cup of ground coffee and silently toasted the unknown hero responsible for sending Arthur the tips.

At lunchtime I fished the small cheap radio out of my shirt drawer and switched on to Radio One. For the next two hours I listened to the old records show, then decided to have Sunday lunch – cheese on toast.

For the rest of the day I lay on the bed with more nostalgia sweeping over me, this time from the cassette player. I thought about dinner with Katie and winning a fortune in the coup.

I spent Monday wishing for Monday evening and, despite the excitement of a man coming to fix the window, the day dragged intolerably.

After leaving work, I bought steak, because it was about the only thing I could cook, potatoes, mushrooms and a few tomatoes. Again, the vegetables were chosen for ease of preparation, not because I particularly liked them. I added a few other things, including a bottle of reasonable red wine, and then set off in Harry's car back to the flat.

I bathed, shaved, polished everywhere I could find to polish, and then set the table. It was lucky I had enough cutlery because I'd never really looked before. I even put on one of the three suits, the beige one – it made me look kind of sophisticated. Then, as I checked the table, it hit me. No glasses! Panic! I didn't have any wine glasses. Well, I'd be lucky to get any at this time of night, so I decided I'd have to make do with what I had.

Feeling like a sixteen-year-old going out on his first date, I drove to the appointed meeting place and waited. And waited. And waited.

At eight-fifteen, I'd been there an hour, and she was forty-five minutes late. I got out of the car for about the tenth time and paced up and down the road. For the second time in a week I wished I had a cigarette, but this time the need was greater. I hadn't smoked since moving to London, mainly because I couldn't afford to, but I could sense my continued abstinence was going to be relatively short-lived.

How long do you wait? I thought. How long before you're sure that she's . . .

'David . . . David . . .' I turned to see Katie running around the corner. 'Oh David, I'm so sorry,' she panted. 'I thought you'd have gone by now. I didn't come back to London until the four o'clock train and it broke down . . .'

'It's all right, you're here now,' I said, laughing. 'I was worried about you.' I wanted to hug her, but decided that wouldn't be a good idea. Instead I opened the car door.

'I didn't realise you had a car.'

'I haven't, this belongs to my boss,' I said honestly.

I drove back to the flat and the evening which started so badly couldn't have gone better. Katie decided that perhaps my flat wasn't too bad by lamplight, and while I cooked she browsed through my music collection.

As well as the pre-recorded variety, I also had a number of tapes that I'd compiled myself from various records begged, bought or borrowed over the years. It was these cassettes which seemed to appeal to Katie the most.

'It must have taken you hours to put all these songs together. Where's your record player?'

'I sold it some time ago.' It was obvious I'd needed the money, but she made no comment.

Over dinner there were no awkward silences and she even made little quips like, 'Could I have another mug of Mouton Cadet?' Everything was perfect, except we still just seemed like good friends. Katie never showed signs of wanting the relationship to progress, and I didn't dare push it in case I lost her altogether.

During the meal I spent a great deal of time studying her. I was already sold on her personality when the evening began, and as we talked the more interested I became. Personality aside, the rest of her wasn't bad either: the shortish brown hair flicked back at the sides revealed a *pretty*, perfectly sculptured face which lit up when she smiled, something she did often. She was petite, around five foot three, with a nice figure, and probably in her mid-twenties. You wouldn't have said she was glamorous in any way, but she was attractive, and I was attracted – very.

Katie asked about my job, and although she didn't understand about bookmakers and boardmen, she easily got the idea that it wasn't the best paid job in the world. I could see the conversation moving towards how I could afford an obviously expensive suit, so I steered it away by telling her a little about my luck with Arthur's tips, and how one day soon I would win a fortune.

It was gone one o'clock when we got into the car. We drove the first five minutes or so in silence; I thought Katie was asleep until I pulled up at a red light and turned to look at her, only to see her looking at me. From her expression I sensed she had been watching me for some time. She smiled and I returned it. I reached down to pull on the handbrake and our fingers touched; that was all it needed. As our skin brushed, our hands automatically linked, and I held hers very tightly. She sighed and put her head on my shoulder. The lights changed, but I wasn't going to risk a change of mood, so I turned left at the lights, and then left again through the entrance of what looked like the car park of a large supermarket. Anyway, it was deserted, and it was dark.

We kissed, gently at first, but followed by much more passion. It sounds corny, but before either of us knew what we were doing, we were making love. It was all totally unreal, but I wasn't about to complain. Then, almost as suddenly as the moment had begun, it was all over and we lay there in each other's arms.

'You must think I'm awful . . .' Her whispered voice sounded upset.

'I was about so say the same thing . . . and I don't think you're awful. In fact, I think I love you.' I hadn't meant to say it, but I did.

Katie gripped me very tightly. 'But you can't, you don't know me.'

'I do, and I do.'

She stroked my face and then held me even tighter.

'Come back to the flat,' I said. 'It's silly going home now.'

She didn't argue. We sat up and rearranged our clothes. Katie looked around; our eyes were barely adjusted to the dark. 'Where on earth are we?' she asked.

I strained to see the sign above the shop entrance. 'I think we're in the Co-op car park.'

She started to laugh. 'Is this what's meant by getting your divi?'

3

For the next three weeks I was ecstatic; I really couldn't remember being happier. Katie didn't actually move in, but she stayed at the flat every night, except for the weekends when she went home to see her mum.

Arthur received two more tips, and to our astonishment the first one was actually beaten, but that wasn't enough to dampen our spirits, particularly when the second horse came in at five to one.

But, happy as I was, I occasionally still had this strange nagging worry over something I couldn't place. I tried to explain it to Jim in the pub when we were celebrating our winner, but he couldn't understand it either.

'It's probably that you're not used to being lucky and you think something's going to happen to spoil it. Perhaps you're concerned about losing that girl of yours; I know you're pretty smitten with her.'

'No, it's nothing to do with Katie. In fact, I'm sure the feeling arrived before she did. But maybe you're right, I am hoping to win a few bob on this coup and it could just be that niggling away at the back of my mind. I think the best thing I can do is forget it and get on with enjoying life.'

The following week, everything happened. On Monday evening Katie informed me she would have the Wednesday and Thursday free, in between changeover of temping jobs. She asked if there was any chance I could have time off to join her; that was easily fixed. Harry said I was entitled to some holiday, and anyway he wanted to take the Friday and Saturday to visit his sister in Leeds, so it would all fit in very nicely.

Wednesday was one of those perfect days I'll always remember. Katie and I played tourists around London and walked all along the embankment from Westminster to Blackfriars, and then up to the top of St Paul's Cathedral. Funny, it doesn't seem that high from the ground looking up, but when you're poised at the top looking down, well, that's an entirely different story.

We were the only people mad enough to be there; hardly surprising since the wind was blowing a gale, and it was trying very hard to rain. Katie went to the railings and looked out over London, with the Thames winding away into forever.

'Come here and look at the view,' she said, holding out her hand.

'Not likely, that railing doesn't look very high to me and it's about three hundred feet down.' I was standing pressed up against the wall like a man waiting for the firing squad, but there I was, and there I was staying.

'Don't be silly,' she teased. 'You can't fall off, not unless you actually climb it.'

The railing looked about four feet high, so I decided to risk it. I took one step forward, lost my nerve, and jumped quickly back to the safety of the wall. Katie gave one of her glowing smiles, and instantly dispelled all doubts I might have had about ever being able to hold my head up as a man again. I led the way slowly down to ground level with knees trembling, but my reputation intact.

The afternoon was spent wandering up Oxford Street, then through Hyde Park, and at around six o'clock we found ourselves standing outside the Hilton.

'Come on,' I said, 'let's go in for a drink.' We walked in as though we owned the place and took the lift to the rooftop cocktail bar. Being quite early it was pretty empty, so we were easily able to get a seat by the window. From there we could gaze down at the world and up at the stars. It was quite impressive. I hoped Katie was impressed.

She was the first to break the silence. 'You're not frightened up here then?'

Me? Frightened? ''Course not,' I replied, pushing back my shoulders and straightening up. The fact that we were behind toughened safety glass could have had something to do with it.

The exotic cocktails were wonderful; expensive, but wonderful. We sipped them slowly through straws; it made them last a bit longer. It seemed I had almost everything: the bar, the drink, and the girl. But there was still one thing missing; I leant over and touched Katie on the arm. 'Do you fancy making love?'

'What, here? In the cocktail bar?'

'Yes, why not?'

'David,' she said in her mock-serious tone, 'this is the Hilton, not the Co-op.'

But the seed was sown. We finished our drinks and went back to the flat.

Later, as I lay in bed staring down at Katie, she suddenly said, 'David, do you realise you haven't mentioned the horses even once today, and you haven't looked at a paper either?'

'I know. Good, isn't it?' But in fact it wasn't good. Had I looked at the racing pages of any newspaper, I wouldn't have been so shocked. I was sure the horse's name would have leapt up off the page at me.

The next morning, Katie discovered we'd run out of cream for the coffee. She decided it was a near catastrophe and quickly dressed to go and fetch some. Very thoughtfully she brought me a copy of the *Sporting Life*.

'Here you are. I can't expect you to go two days without the horses,' she said, throwing the paper onto the bed where I was sitting. Usually I'd look at the headlines first, but since it landed with the front cover against the bedclothes, it was the back page that caught my eye.

My gasp could probably have been heard outside. Katie must have said something, but I didn't hear. She put a concerned arm around my shoulders, and followed my gaze to the photograph of a rather glamorous woman holding the reins of a horse and being presented with a trophy.

Katie lifted the paper off the bed and read the caption out loud. 'Mrs Elaine Ellerton, wife of the chairman of Ellerton Press (Wolverhampton) Limited, is presented with the Severn Trophy following the success of the company's horse, Ellerton Express, at Worcester yesterday.' She looked at me and spoke again. 'Darling, what's wrong? Your face is white; this wasn't your coup thing, was it?'

I recovered my voice. 'No, it wasn't my coup thing.'

'Do you know the girl?'

'You might say that.'

'What is she, who is she?' Katie was beginning to sound uneasy.

I hesitated for a second and then decided the truth had to be the best way out of this one. 'She's the reason I live in a grotty bedsitter and work as a boardman's assistant.'

Katie held both my hands tightly. 'I don't understand, David. Tell me what you mean.'

I hesitated again. 'You won't like it.'

'I don't care, please tell me.'

I stood up and walked slowly over to the cooker, where I poured out the two cups of coffee Katie had started to make. I took them over to the bed, and this time it was my turn to put my arm around her. 'It's not a pretty story, and it doesn't have a happy ending . . .' I paused, '. . . unless you're it.'

She looked up and kissed my cheek, but I noticed the tears beginning to well in her eyes. She put her arms around my neck and her head on my shoulder. 'Tell me, please.'

I took a deep breath, left my head against hers and started. 'I used to work for Ellerton Press; in fact I joined them straight from school with the grand total of three O-levels. Even as general dogsbody, it was a nice place to work. The owner, old man Ellerton, had run the place for near on fifty years and most of the staff had been there almost as long as he had. There was little in the way of promotion prospects, but at that time I didn't really care, as long as I got paid each week.'

My throat felt dry, but I didn't want to disturb Katie by reaching for the coffee, so I swallowed hard and continued. 'Anyway, after I'd been there for almost twelve months, everything changed. Old man Ellerton died and George, his son, took over. George must have been about forty, and he was a real bastard, nothing at all like his father. Up until then he'd been a successful accountant with his own business in Birmingham, but no sooner was the coffin lid nailed shut than he sold up and put the money into Ellerton Press. To give him his due, he obviously knew what he was doing, because over the years he built the company up from a small local operation into what it is today, a substantial group with fourteen papers. He also holds the advertising contracts for most of the large corporate accounts in the Midlands. In a nutshell, George Ellerton became an extremely wealthy and powerful man in a comparatively short space of time.'

Katie looked up. 'He just sounds like a good businessman to me.'

'Oh, he's that all right, but it's just the way he did things. He'd only been in charge for ten days when he sacked five men who'd been with the company for at least twenty years. And when I say sacked, I mean sacked, not made redundant or offered early retirement. They hadn't done anything wrong, their faces just didn't fit, so he saw no point in paying them.'

'But you can't just get rid of people like that,' Katie interrupted. 'There are laws against it.'

'Well, he did, called it incompetence, and Ellerton defied anyone to prove differently. Let's face it, Katie; if you were fifty and led a fairly sheltered, uncomplicated life, how would you feel about trying to win some sort of legal battle against the likes of Ellerton?' She nodded, and I continued. 'Well, that set the ground rules; he ruled by terror and everyone was duly terrified. I remembered thinking it was like being back at school; if Ellerton appeared in any of the offices, everything would go quiet and all heads would be down working – just as if the headmaster had walked into the classroom.'

'But what about you? Did it affect you at all?'

'Funnily enough, I was one of the few existing staff who came out of it well, but it took a long time. After doing nothing very much for a few years, I suddenly found myself in the Advertising Sales Department because half the staff were off with flu. After two weeks I'd sold more than most did in a month, and what's more, I enjoyed every minute of it. I was sorry to go back to my usual mundane routine when the sick parade returned, but I'd only just sat down at my desk when I was summoned to His Master's presence. I'd never been in Ellerton's office before, in fact I'd hardly ever spoken to the man, and suddenly there I was, standing in front of him; he didn't ask me to sit.'

'What was he like, to look at, I mean?'

'Oh, about six foot, greying hair, thin. I know I'm biased, but he looked malicious, a bit like a hawk.'

Katie took my cup of cold coffee and refilled it.

'Well, he told me that as I seemed to have a sort of flair for it, my new role in Ellerton Press would be selling advertising contracts to major companies, a sort of sales rep. "Go out and get business, big business, lots of it." There was no "this is how you do it, David, my boy", and it was obvious that, if I wasn't successful, then I needn't bother showing my face in the office again. He didn't offer any salary increase, but he did agree to pay commission. I remembered thinking I'd be out of a job in a month, but I wasn't. Truth was, I was extremely good at it, and in fact I was soon coming out with virtually three times my former salary; but almost better than the money was the freedom. Nobody asked where I was going or what I was doing; as long as I brought in the business no one cared.'

Katie looked as if she knew what was coming next, and I didn't disappoint her. 'So, I'd arrange my meetings in Nottingham when it was Nottingham races, my Warwick appointments would surprisingly coincide with Warwick races, and so on. No one in the office knew I liked the horses, and even if they had, they'd never have noticed my schedule.'

Katie was glaring disapprovingly, but remembering the good bits of my previous employment had lifted my spirits a little.

'Katie darling, it wasn't the racing that was my downfall; there's much worse to come.'

She smiled a worried smile and I took her in my arms. I had thoughts of a short interlude for lovemaking, but she read my mind and the idea was instantly aborted.

'Anyway, I won an attractive contract from a company in Walsall, and Ellerton decided he'd invite the Marketing Director to a party in his home, obviously hoping for a much larger contract next time around. Ellerton reluctantly decided I'd better be there too to look after the guy. He needn't have worried, because this particular Marketing Director marketed his way rather rapidly through the whisky, and only an hour into the party I poured him into a taxi and sent him home a happy man. I was looking for Ellerton to tell him all was well and that I was going home, when I met his wife.

'I'd never thought about George Ellerton being married. I suppose it's one of those things most people take for granted about other people, but it never occurred to me that he would be married to such a . . . well . . .' I struggled for the right words, so Katie helped me out.

'It's all right, I can see she's a very attractive woman. You don't have to spare my feelings; I can take it.' She spoke in a glib, half-serious manner, but I could sense she was starting to get upset. To say Elaine Ellerton was very attractive was an understatement, and even though the picture in the paper made her look very good indeed, by no stretch of the imagination did it do her justice. In my view, a view shared by most of the men who knew her, she could only be described as stunning, absolutely stunning.

Katie interrupted my thoughts by picking up the *Sporting Life*. She looked more closely at the photograph. 'How old is she?'

'She'll be twenty-eight now.' I wished afterwards I'd pretended to think for a second, but by then it was too late.

'She doesn't look it.' Katie put the paper back down on the bed and stared up at me for a second or two before speaking. 'So you had an affair.'

'Well . . . er, yes.'

'And hubby found out.'

'Well . . . er . . . not exactly. At the party we talked for about half an hour and seemed to get on well together. I mentioned I had a meeting in Coventry the next day and she said she was lunching there, so we arranged to meet for coffee. It progressed from there.

'Elaine came from an ordinary background but was determined to marry someone wealthy. I suppose with her looks she had a pretty good chance of succeeding. When we met, she'd been married to Ellerton for five years. I'm sure I wasn't the first she'd had an affair with and I don't suppose I'll be the last. She wasn't too keen on George, but she had no intention of rocking the boat; she liked the money and the lifestyle too much.'

'She sounds like a right bitch,' Katie couldn't help but say.

'I don't mean to make her sound like that, because she wasn't. She was just a nice girl who should have been a model or a film star. Instead she married George.' Katie was still looking at me with disbelief in her eyes. 'Honestly, Katie, I'm not making excuses for her . . .'

'What did George think of her?' Katie interrupted, wanting to change the line of conversation.

'Elaine used to say he treated her like he treated everything in life, a possession.' The more I spoke, the more I could see Katie getting jealous and, to be honest, I quite liked it; it showed she really did care for me. She had never told me she loved me and I always felt she was holding back emotionally, so a little rearing of the green monster was a good sign. Still, there was no point in upsetting her unnecessarily, so I took her hands and told her I loved her more than a hundred Elaine Ellertons. I meant it too.

'Oh David . . .' I felt sure she was about to say something nice to me, something I wanted to hear, but then she changed her mind and the moment was lost. 'Finish your tale.'

'Well, surprisingly enough, Elaine liked horse-racing. She used to go with her father when she was young, and when I suggested going one day she jumped at it. She never gambled, she just loved the atmosphere and the occasion. We often joked about getting George to buy her a racehorse, but she said he'd never had even the slightest interest.

'Anyway, one of the bonuses of having Elaine was her car. She had a beautiful silver BMW, and since my old car was literally falling apart we used to go to my meetings in hers, and then I'd charge the company for petrol, which of course George paid for anyway . . .'

Katie was shaking her head, obviously disapproving again, so I held up my hands as a sign of surrender. 'I know it wasn't exactly honest, but he deserved it. Anyway, this went on for almost a year, then disaster struck. We were on our way back from the races in the BMW when we had an accident. Poetic justice, I suppose: we ran into a horsebox!'

Katie gave a half-hearted laugh.

'It wasn't funny,' I said, trying to keep the mood light. 'It could have been very nasty. We whizzed around a corner at about sixty, only to find a horsebox right in front of us. Elaine tried to avoid it, but we clipped the side, spun around and ploughed through a fence.

'The next thing I knew was when I woke up that evening in hospital, with George Ellerton's very angry face staring down at me. Fortunately two nurses and a doctor made him leave, said I was suffering from concussion, but even more fortunate, Elaine was kept in overnight for observation, so we were able to concoct our story together. Not that it made much difference; George wasn't stupid – most accountants can add two and two. We swore blind Elaine was only giving me a lift to my meeting after we'd accidentally met earlier, but all Ellerton could say was that he'd see to it I'd never work again. And that was the last I saw of either of them.'

'How long ago was that?' Katie asked.

'Fifteen months, and he was dead right: I haven't been able to get a proper job since. Initially I thought being such a super salesman I'd easily find work, but since Ellerton Press held all my sales records I had nothing to show in the way of achievements, and my three O-levels have never exactly got people excited. Even worse, Ellerton had contacts everywhere and no company in the Midlands would touch me. Even when I came to London, he managed to put the mockers on a couple of likely looking job prospects.' I shrugged my shoulders, beginning to feel a bit sorry for myself after such an obvious tale of woe. 'So here I sit holding the envious position of boardman's assistant, and having the grand total of two hundred pounds to my name.'

Katie obviously had no sympathy, but she did manage a smile. 'You should have applied to the Co-op; you're good there.'

The following day was Friday, and Katie went off to her next assignment and then home to mum. I went off to H. Greenaway Turf Accountant.

As I walked through the drizzle, I sang an old Colin Blunstone song I'd been playing whilst we were dressing. I thought that when I eventually won the fortune (I was becoming increasingly confident about winning) I'd buy myself one of those personal cassette players so I could have music as I walked. But for now it was my singing or nothing. I decided nothing was better, and thought about Katie. Funny how I felt so much happier now, and yet I still longed for Mondays. If I got myself a proper job I wouldn't have to work on Saturdays; that way I could perhaps go and meet Katie's mum. Finding another job was suddenly becoming much more important.

I arrived at the shop and remembered Harry was away until Monday, so I expected a bit of confusion without him there to marshal the troops. What I did not expect was to be grabbed excitedly by both Jim and Arthur the second I walked through the door.

'It's here, look!' Arthur shouted, and rammed an envelope into my hand. I shivered and looked at the buff brown paper, then back to my two excited compatriots. Slowly I took out the letter; my hands were shaking as I read:

Dear Mr Clifford,
The time has now arrived for my final bet. This is the certain winner I promised:
 BRASS LOCK, SATURDAY 2 p.m., ASCOT. STAKE, £500 WIN
 As I explained in my first letter, there is no doubt the horse will win, so therefore feel free to have a substantial wager yourself. You will, of course, be entitled to your ten per cent of my winnings as usual. My only request is that you spread the stake around a few bookmakers . . .

I looked up at Jim. 'But isn't Brass Lock up against Towerstack and The Reserved Flyer? He hasn't got a cat in hell's chance.'

Towerstack was thought by many to be the best three-mile chaser in the country. He was only just beaten in the last few strides of the Cheltenham Gold Cup the previous March, but had been off the course since then due to an injury sustained in the race.

'I know it looks a difficult race for Brass Lock to win, but finish reading the letter,' came Jim's confident reply.

I read on:

I realise the selection will surprise you since the opposition is formidable. I therefore feel a brief explanation is necessary.
There will probably be only four runners in the race. The favourite will be Towerstack, and under normal circumstances he would win it with ease. However, I am reliably informed that Towerstack has not yet fully recovered from his injury and his trainer is giving him the run purely to test his leg; he is nowhere near fit enough to win.

The second favourite will be The Reserved Flyer; you may recall he won the three-mile novice chase at the Cheltenham Festival. If you look at his form, you will notice his jumping is more than a little suspect. Take my word for it, his jumping will be extremely suspect during this race.

The fourth horse in the field, Catclaw, has no chance whatsoever, so that only leaves Brass Lock. He is extremely fit, fit enough to win. I appreciate that, under normal circumstances, Brass Lock would be out of his class against Towerstack and The Reserved Flyer, but these circumstances are not normal.

Thank you for your help in this most profitable of ventures.

C. A. Davidson

P.S. You will of course destroy this letter.

I looked at Jim; we both looked at Arthur.

'The bugger's fixed it, hasn't he?' Jim said. 'He's fixed the bloody race.'

'I don't know,' I said, shaking my head. 'I mean, how do you fix a race of this class?'

'It's easy. Catclaw has never been in the first three in his life, so he's no chance. Towerstack is only half fit, so that rules him out. All our man's got to do is nobble The Reserved Flyer and he's done it. After all, Brass Lock's a fairly reasonable horse, a safe jumper – okay, so he's a bit one-paced, but he's won half a dozen races, hasn't he?'

Arthur went to make the coffee and I looked at the letter again. 'This Davidson guy is taking one hell of a chance putting it all down in writing. Why didn't he simply write "Brass Lock, £500 to win" like he did with the other tips?'

'I wondered that, but I think he wants Arthur to have a good bet on it himself, set him and his missus up financially. After all, he did his homework so he knows Arthur hasn't exactly had a prosperous life, and the whole world likes him. I mean, you couldn't meet a nicer old man.'

'I suppose you're right. If it hadn't been spelt out in the letter, Arthur could hardly have been expected to put out much of his own money against that opposition.'

Arthur returned with the coffee and I handed him back his letter.

'Well, lad, this is it, eh?' he chuckled. 'We're going to be rich.'

The day dragged intolerably; I couldn't stop thinking about Brass Lock. It seemed strange that for the last five weeks I had been waiting for the day to arrive, and now the moment was close I almost wished it wasn't. I suppose it was only natural, what with all the excitement in the lead up, tomorrow would be something of an anti-climax. But that was silly, because when the race was over I would still have Katie, and I would be considerably more wealthy. But how much more wealthy? That was the problem.

As evening approached, I slipped out of the shop and bought an *Evening Standard*. My excitement was so great that I stood in the drizzle and turned immediately to the second to last page. There was the Ascot programme for the following day, and sure enough in the two o'clock there were only four runners. Towerstack was the odds on favourite, The Reserved Flyer was seven to four, Brass Lock was eight to one, with Catclaw thirty-threes.

The odds seemed about right and as I walked back to the shop I slowly reviewed my financial situation. All I had in the world was £200, and at eight to one that would give me £1,600 profit, less tax. Not exactly enough to set the world alight, but it wasn't to be sneezed at either. If someone had told me six months ago I was going to win £1,600, I would have been absolutely ecstatic, yet now here I was thinking it wasn't enough. Funny old life! I suppose knowing an eight-to-one certainty and not having enough stake to make a killing was disappointing. It never occurred to me that if it lost it would set me back months. It never occurred to me that it might lose.

As I reached the shop, two ideas sprang into my mind simultaneously; it must have been my quota for the month. Firstly, I would go to Ascot because I might get better odds than eight to one on the course, and also I wouldn't have to pay tax on my winnings. The other idea would take a little more planning.

As I walked back through the door, I was besieged by Arthur and Jim, both wanting to see the paper. Like me, they were pleased at the prospect of an eight-to-one winner. Fortunately the day's racing was over and the punters had cleared off home. We hadn't been very busy all day; the rain had kept most of them away.

We locked the shop door to avoid any last-minute stragglers and then we all just stood, gazing at the paper, pound signs flashing up before our eyes. I decided it was a good time to suggest Plan A. I had no intention of mentioning Plan B.

'What do you think about me going to Ascot tomorrow, Jim?'

'I don't suppose it would matter. 'Arry won't be here and we could always say you were sick.'

'I could put your bets on for you, perhaps get a better price and save the tax. What do you think?' I directed my question to Arthur.

'Well, I don't mind you going, keep you out of my bloody hair – you'll be unbearable tomorrow,' he joked. 'But I think I'll put my own money on, that way it's my responsibility.'

'Arthur's right,' Jim interrupted. 'You go by all means, you'd only be a nuisance here, but I'll put my money on and I'll put our ace tipster's five hundred quid on too. That way he'll get the starting price and there won't be any problems.'

That suited me fine; I didn't really want the responsibility of putting anyone else's money on, and in a situation like this I certainly would-n't have wanted someone putting my stake on for me. Arthur and Jim decided they were each going to put £100 on Brass Lock and, not wish-ing to appear greedy, I said I would probably do the same.

Arthur looked tired so we told him to go home and I gave Jim a hand to cash up. When we finished, Jim locked the money in the safe and put the key in his pocket, then offered to help me sweep up. I told him not to worry; it was a challenging task but I thought I could tackle it single-handed. Briefly translated, it meant I was in no hurry to get back to the flat.

'Go on, Jim, clear off home to your missus. I can put the catch down on the door as easy as you.'

'Well, make sure you switch off the lights,' he joked.

So there I was, all alone in the shop. I made sure the front door was locked and then went into the back office. I moved the table and felt along the wall for the loose brick, removing it slowly. There it was, Plan B: Harry's 'in case of emergency' 300 quid!

Back at the flat I carefully counted my stake: £500 in total. I tried not to think about 'borrowing' Harry's money; after all I could replace it when Brass Lock won and no one would be any the wiser. I didn't dare think about what would happen if it lost. The thought of having to face the man who had given me a job and lent me his car, only to tell him I'd stolen his money, was unthinkable. So I didn't think about it.

But I dreamt about it. I dreamt about winning, I dreamt about los-ing, in fact when I woke up I felt I hadn't been to sleep at all. I put on the kettle to make some coffee and then realised it was only half-past six. I tried to go back to sleep but it was impossible, so I got dressed and went out to buy a *Sporting Life*.

It was still dark as I walked down to the newsagent's and I suddenly realised it wasn't raining. I couldn't be sure if that was a good sign or not – lately most good things seemed to have happened to me in the rain. Still, I took comfort in the thought that it was bound to be rain-ing again by the afternoon. I bought the racing paper and stood under a street light to read the feature article on the race in question. Each of the journalists was fairly certain Towerstack would win comfortably, but of course they didn't know what I knew. I also became more con-fident when I read that, due to injury, Towerstack wasn't going to be ridden by his usual jockey, but by one of the young apprentices from the stable. The newspaper's expert felt the choice of jockey would have no bearing on the result, saying that Towerstack would win if his granny rode it. My view was that the trainer probably thought the horse would-n't win anyway, and he might as well give one of his apprentices the ride.

A milk float came slowly to a stop a few feet ahead of me, so I bought a small carton of double cream and went back to the flat.

I tried everything: I played my favourite cassettes, I put on the radio, I read, but it was hopeless. I couldn't concentrate on anything for more than five minutes; my mind kept wandering back to Brass Lock. At about ten, I decided to make my way to Ascot.

I stepped outside the front door and my nagging doubt was instantly there. Instinctively I thrust my hand into my overcoat pocket where the £500 lay; I kept my hand on it all the way to Ascot.

The journey was reasonably easy. I caught the tube to Waterloo and then the train to Ascot. I arrived just after twelve and my nagging worry came with me all the way. I decided it was only natural I should be concerned; after all, in just over two hours' time it would be all or nothing. In fact, all, or much less than nothing.

There was an hour to kill before the first race, so I wandered around the few shops which backed onto the racecourse and made up Ascot village. I had been to Ascot once before with Elaine, but I hadn't really noticed the shops then. This time the only thought that really struck me was that Ascot itself was only there courtesy of the racecourse. I walked past a very nice gallery selling expensive portraits of racehorses. I admired the one to the side of the window on offer at £550. I thought that on my way back I could buy six of them if I wanted; I wouldn't, of course, but it was nice to think I could.

I paid to go into the Tattersalls. Most racecourses have three viewing areas: the members' enclosure is the most expensive and offers the best view; the Tattersalls is usually not far behind as far as viewing goes, but because it's a few pounds cheaper it gets more crowded. The third area is known as the Silver Ring at Ascot, or 'the course' on many other tracks, and is usually half the price of the Tattersalls. Like most things in life, you get what you pay for. Having said that, I had been to some courses where the Silver Ring was quite good, but I chose the Tattersalls at Ascot because, like the members' enclosure, it gave access to the parade ring.

I looked at my watch for the thousandth time; it was a quarter to one, fifteen minutes before the first race. The stands were beginning to fill up, but I doubted if there would be a big crowd; the dark skies and cold wind would put most people off and having four out of the six races televised didn't help. Still, no doubt Ascot's management were more than happy with the deal struck on TV rights. I wondered how many people, both on the course and at home, had money on Towerstack; quite a few, I suspected. I was sorry they were going to be disappointed.

The first two races came and went, and if a latecomer had asked me what had won either race, I couldn't have told him. I didn't even have a bet; I just stood with my right hand firmly wedged inside my coat pocket and looked at the races without taking anything in.

After the second race, I made my way down to the parade ring and got a good place right on the rails. However, by the time the first of the four runners came into view the steps were packed solid; no doubt most of them were there to get a good look at the likely winner of next year's Gold Cup. I looked around at the sea of faces and wondered if Mr Davidson was amongst them. I wondered if he felt like I did: positively sick.

· The first horse to come in was The Reserved Flyer, followed closely by Brass Lock and Catclaw. The thing that was instantly noticeable was the size of The Reserved Flyer; he was enormous, in fact he made the other two look like ponies. As Brass Lock passed by, I wanted to tell him how much his winning meant to me, but I decided the two-and-a-half miles and sixteen or so fences would be difficult enough without having to contend with my worries.

After a couple of minutes, Towerstack strode into the ring like a true prima donna making an entrance. Every head turned to look at him and, as if in acknowledgement, he swished his tail and jabbed back his head with a haughty superiority. He paraded apart from the other horses, like aristocracy amongst peasants. I wondered if he knew he wasn't fit. He certainly looked fit, but then my untrained eye couldn't tell a Derby winner from a donkey; even Catclaw looked good to me.

I pushed through the crowds around the parade ring and walked briskly back to the area in front of the grandstand, where most of the bookmakers had their pitches. 'Seven to four The Flyer,' one was shouting, trying to encourage a little business for the second favourite. I walked along the lines of bookies, studying the odds. All of them were virtually the same. Towerstack was odds-on favourite, The Reserved Flyer seven to four against, Brass Lock eight to one, and Catclaw's price varied from thirty-threes to fifty to one. I took a couple of minutes to look for a better price, but eights was as good as I was going to get, so I approached one of the more prosperous looking bookmakers, took my right hand out of my pocket and held up the wad of notes. 'Five hundred, Brass Lock.'

I didn't know what I expected, but he simply took the money and stuffed it in his satchel without even counting it. 'Four grand to a half, ticket seventy-one,' was all he said.

I looked at the orange-coloured ticket bearing the bookmaker's name and the number 071 printed in large black characters. Then I walked up a dozen steps and found a good vantage point in the stand.

'*The runners for the third race on their way down to the start,*' the commentator's voice boomed out over the public address system. It was then I realised I had forgotten my binoculars. My binoculars, like my cassette player, were one of the few items left from my more affluent days, and it showed what a state I must have been in to go to the races without them. Still, with only four runners, I wouldn't have much difficulty in making them out.

The horses emerged onto the course to my far left and began cantering down to the two-and-a-half mile start. I would have liked my binoculars to get a close-up of Dennis Earl, The Reserved Flyer's jockey. He was one of the top ten jump jockeys in the country and I was surprised to think he would deliberately throw the race. But then again, jump jockeys don't get paid anything like their counterparts on the flat, and if Mr Davidson offered a couple of thousand for a jockey to fall off a horse that was known to be a dicey jumper anyway, then it would probably be hard to refuse.

'The horses are at the start,' the commentator's voice boomed again.

My right hand was back in my coat pocket, only this time gripping the bookmaker's ticket.

'Under starter's orders . . .' I took an involuntary gasp of cold air, *'. . . and they're off.'*

There were shouts of encouragement from the crowd as the four competitors started virtually together, but as they ran to the first jump The Reserved Flyer went off in his customary trail-blazing manner. He flew over the fence and quickly opened up a lead of five or six lengths from Towerstack and Brass Lock, with Catclaw already lagging well behind.

The race commentator took up the story:

'Coming up to the fourth fence and it's The Reserved Flyer by six lengths from Towerstack who's four lengths in front of Brass Lock, another ten lengths to Catclaw.'

The horses were making their way into the straight and, although it looked as if The Reserved Flyer was a fair way in front, I wasn't worried because I expected him to fall somewhere out in the country. Ascot racecourse is triangular in shape, with the grandstands and winning post at the base of the triangle. I expected Dennis Earl to execute his fall as far away from the stands as possible.

'Coming past the stands for the first time with one complete circuit left to race and it's The Reserved Flyer by six lengths from Towerstack, these two have now drawn twelve lengths in front of Brass Lock, with Catclaw already becoming tailed off.'

As the horses passed me, I had my first feeling that something was wrong. It wasn't that Brass Lock was a fair way behind, it was just that Towerstack looked remarkably good. They had run about three-quarters of a mile and, rather than looking as though he might falter at any minute, Towerstack looked raring to go; in fact, his young apprentice jockey was having difficulty in restraining him.

'*On their way down the far side, with eight fences still to jump, the order remains the same, The Reserved Flyer by six lengths from Towerstack, but these two have now drawn well clear of Brass Lock, with Catclaw tailed off.*'

In spite of the cold I felt beads of perspiration forming on my forehead. Something was disastrously wrong. There was about half a mile left to run, and Brass Lock was at least twenty-five lengths behind the second horse, and the jockey seemed to have accepted third place. He had stopped giving him the occasional crack with the whip and was simply riding him along. Meanwhile, the leading two were increasing their pace with every stride.

'*Making their way to the third last fence, The Reserved Flyer holding his six-length lead over Towerstack, these two well clear.*'

I stood mesmerised, just staring across the course at Brass Lock; he was now almost a fence behind the leading two and had no chance whatsoever. What a mess! I couldn't even go back to work; Harry would soon discover the money had gone, and that would be that. I doubted if he would involve the police, but it would probably be better if he did. At least I would have a cell to live in, because I wouldn't be able to pay the rent on the flat. What a mess! What a fool! I felt a ringing sensation in my ears and the stands began to sway. I thought I was going to pass out so I grabbed the handrail to steady myself; a few deep breaths and I was okay again – well, as okay as I was likely to be.

The crowd began to shout and cheer. The Reserved Flyer had jumped the second last still six lengths in front of Towerstack, but on the run up to the last fence, the young jockey gave Towerstack a little tap with the whip and they switched into overdrive. Towerstack's acceleration was staggering; there was a roar from the crowd as he cruised up on the inside of the leading horse. Throughout the whole race that was the apprentice's only mistake; he had the whole of Ascot's racecourse to choose from, but he took Towerstack through the small gap between The Reserved Flyer and the rails. Dennis Earl sensed Towerstack's presence at his mount's hind quarters and tried to regain some of his advantage by getting a big jump out of The Reserved Flyer at the last fence.

The consequences were amazing. The Reserved Flyer took off well behind the fence and almost cleared it, but his hind legs hit the top hard, causing his front legs to collapse on landing. Towerstack was in the air by this time and, although he cleared the fence without any difficulty, he couldn't avoid landing right on top of The Reserved Flyer and being brought down in a heap.

Both jockeys lay dazed on the ground as Brass Lock cantered up to the fence, skipped over it and trotted up to the winning post.

4

Most of the punters were either making their way to bars to drown their sorrows (after all, no one would have been mad enough to put money on Brass Lock) or to view the horses for the next race. I simply stood motionless, riveted to the spot. One hand was clutching the rail as if fused by an electric current, the other was still firmly rooted in my pocket, guarding the betting slip. Summoning up the few fragments of courage I had left, I pulled out the crumpled piece of paper and studied it carefully. Number 071 was now worth a fortune, at least in my terms, so I did my best to straighten it out.

I was still feeling sick and decidedly shaky as I forcefully prised my hand from the rail and checked my pocket for change. Almost £3. A glass of whisky definitely wouldn't go amiss. There would be no point in trying to pick up my winnings yet – the bookmaker certainly wouldn't pay out before the horses had weighed in, so I joined the crowds and made a move towards the nearest bar. On my way down the steps, I noticed the bookies putting up their umbrellas. It was raining.

I bought a small whisky and also a packet of cigarettes. I was annoyed with myself for giving in to the urge, but I was desperate and felt the situation warranted a lapse in discipline.

I drank the Scotch in two gulps, and after a few puffs on the cigarette I felt my sanity returning. The public address system announced the horses had weighed in, so I walked out into the rain, found my bookmaker and handed him the ticket.

'Ticket seventy-one,' he growled, 'four-and-a-half grand to the luckiest bastard in the country.' I just smiled; second luckiest, I thought, and gratefully stuffed the money into every pocket I had.

I lit another cigarette and gazed out over Ascot heath. The rain was pelting down and everyone except the bookmakers had taken shelter in the stands and bars. I felt the notes of various denominations in my pockets and began to realise just how lucky I had been.

But what had gone wrong? There was no way Brass Lock should have won that race. Dennis Earl obviously had every intention of winning it on The Reserved Flyer, and Towerstack was undoubtedly at peak fitness. I had won £4,000 by pure fluke.

I wondered about C. A. Davidson. By now he would be a very wealthy man indeed, again by fluke. Someone had given him totally wrong information, and even under the circumstances I doubted if he would be too happy with his informants.

Still, why worry? I had won; so had Jim, Arthur and Mr Davidson. I subconsciously patted my pockets and decided there was no point in staying for the last three races. Apart from anything else, it was a bit risky hanging around with over four grand in readies, so I left the track and walked briskly to the railway station.

I was in luck for the second time that day. A train pulled in almost as soon as I set foot on the platform, and I took a seat in one of those largish compartments. It wasn't until the two men got in about thirty seconds later that I realised I was the only person in there. Two men walking into a railway compartment is an everyday occurrence, but suddenly I felt very much at risk. It wasn't the fact that I was carrying so much money, it was that same old nagging, worried feeling, only magnified a hundred times. The two men sat in the seat directly behind me. With all the carriage to choose from, why on earth should they sit there? I felt myself starting to panic, and then the train jerked as it was about to move out. No escape now.

Suddenly there was shouting and laughter on the platform, together with the sound of running feet. The train was just starting to move as the door was thrown open and a party of people almost fell into the carriage.

There were six of them, three of each sex, all in their early twenties and all a little tipsy. They sank into the set of six seats on the opposite side of the compartment. They were all gasping for breath and the girls were giggling.

'Come on, darling,' a blonde girl said to one of the men, 'where's the bubbly? I'm absolutely desperate.'

'Yes, come on, Geoffrey, get it out,' the others chimed in.

Geoffrey got to his feet and started to undo his zip. The girls shrieked.

'No, no, the champers, darling!' the blonde screamed. 'I'll have some of that later.' The carriage erupted with their laughter again.

Geoffrey reached into a holdall by his feet and produced two bottles of Moet et Chandon and some plastic beakers. The other five cheered, and I breathed a huge sigh of relief; I had never been so glad to have such riotous company. There was a sudden bang as a champagne cork shot off down the train, and everyone fought to get their beaker under the expensive flow.

'I say, old boy, care to join us in a glass?'

I realised with a certain amount of surprise that Geoffrey was addressing me.

'Oh yes, do,' chirped one of the girls. 'It's my birthday and I'll be awfully offended if you don't.'

Well, put like that, how could I refuse? To save Geoffrey getting up to pour the drink, I moved into the seat opposite mine; that way I was facing the two men who were causing me so much concern. I couldn't see them too well, just their heads over the top of the seats, but their reaction was quite astonishing. They had been talking quietly between themselves until they noticed me switch seats, then they quickly got up and moved to the other end of the carriage, sitting down with their backs towards me. Very strange indeed.

I leaned back in my seat and took a sip of champagne, then raised my beaker to the birthday girl and wished her many happy returns. That sparked an outbreak of 'Happy Birthday To You' from the rest of the group, and I sang along with them, deciding it was silly to be so paranoid about the two men.

Still, I wasn't taking any chances so, as the train pulled into Waterloo, I leapt out of the door and ran down the platform like an Olympic sprinter after a gold medal. Thrusting my ticket into the outstretched hand of the British Rail man at the barrier, I fled across the station concourse and into a waiting taxi.

'Trafalgar Square, please,' I shouted breathlessly. As the cab pulled away, I craned my neck to look through the back window, but there was no sign of the two men.

The taxi crossed Waterloo Bridge and weaved its way down the Strand. I sat back in the seat and began to relax a little, hoping I'd remembered to say cheerio to the birthday party.

'Anywhere in particular you want dropping, guv?' the driver asked pleasantly.

'Over by the Post Office.' I pointed across to the other side of the Square. 'And would you mind waiting for me, please?'

'No problem, guv, you're paying the bill.'

I gave a self-satisfied smile; funny to think of me actually being able to afford to take a taxi these days.

Trafalgar Square is in the unique position of having a Post Office open all day Saturday and all day Sunday, as well as most hours in the week. In my more affluent days, I had banked with Girobank through the Post Office network. I hadn't used my account for the last six months or so, mainly because the Giro people get a bit upset if you take money out when you don't have any in, but this seemed like a good day to make a deposit.

The taxi stopped as near as the driver could get it to the building and, as if treading on hot coals, I crossed the wet pavement in four strides and skidded in.

There were very few customers about, so I walked straight up to a counter clerk and pushed the bundles of money under the glass partition. As I completed the paying-in slip in the back of my once-redundant cheque book, I couldn't help but think how it must have been quite common for people to pay in amounts of £4,000 on a Saturday afternoon, because my counter clerk didn't bat an eyelid. He just counted the money, stamped my cheque book and carried on chatting to one of his colleagues about Queens Park Rangers' chances of winning their match.

I leapt back over the red-hot coals and into the taxi, giving the driver the address of H. Greenaway Turf Accountant. I had banked all the money except Harry's £300, plus £100 in pocket money for myself. I now felt considerably better; in fact I felt decidedly happy. I just wished Katie could be there when I got home. Home? Was I beginning to think of that grotty bedsit as home? Soon I'd get myself a proper job, use my winnings as a deposit on a flat and persuade Katie to marry me. Oh Katie, how I long for Monday to see you; what a lot there is to tell you.

It was gone five when the taxi dropped me outside Harry's shop. The door was locked, but the lights were still on, so I gave the window a couple of sharp taps. No reply, so I rapped again.

'We're closed,' Jim's anything-but-dulcet tones yelled.

'It's me, you berk,' I shouted back.

I heard the sound of feet rushing across the floor, then the door was flung open and Jim's smiling face beckoned me in. Jim and Sylvia, together with Arthur and his wife, were sitting in the front of the shop drinking coffee, so I took the opportunity to slip into the office and make myself a cup. Once there, I quickly slid the £300 back into Harry's hiding place, made the coffee and went back to the others.

'Bloody lucky, weren't we?' Arthur said.

'Too right,' I answered, before Jim could.

Arthur's wife turned to me. 'Do you know, David, Arthur and me have got almost one thousand pounds. We've never had so much money in our lives. I don't know what we're going to do with it.'

'You enjoy it, Mrs C.,' Sylvia said, 'we're certainly going to.'

I smiled at Arthur's wife. She seemed totally bemused by it all. I supposed that having lived hand to mouth for so many years, the whole episode would be overwhelming for the Cliffords, but I was pleased for them, and very pleased for myself.

'Listen, you lot,' I said, gaining their attention, 'how about Sunday lunch on me tomorrow?'

Sylvia and Mrs C. started to object, but I raised my hand to silence them. 'No buts, I insist. You're all having lunch with me. I owe you and Jim stacks of meals,' I said, turning to Sylvia, 'and Arthur, if it hadn't been for you giving me the information, I wouldn't have won a bean. So, that's settled, you're all dining with me. Okay?'

'Okay,' they replied in unison.

'It's very nice of you, David,' Sylvia said, 'but where are you taking us?'

'A good point,' I conceded. 'Any ideas, because I don't really know anywhere?'

'What about that new place by us,' Mrs C. suggested. 'It looks very nice and I don't think it's expensive.'

We all agreed and arranged to meet in the bar at noon the following day. Arthur and his good lady went home, as did Sylvia, saying that she had to put Jim's tea on. Jim and I decided to go for a quick drink.

'Here's to winners,' I said, raising my glass, 'as lucky as they may be.'

'Lucky wasn't the word for it. I'll bet you were having bloody kittens watching Brass Lock getting further and further behind.'

'I was,' I replied truthfully. 'What was it like on the television?'

'Well, to start with, if we hadn't put our bloody money on in the morning, we probably wouldn't have backed it. Firstly they interviewed Dennis Earl, and he was saying how they'd been schooling The Reserved Flyer over fences for the past few months, and how he was now almost foot perfect. Then when the horses were in the parade ring, Richard Pitman said he thought Towerstack looked very well and very fit, and he should know, he was a top bloody jockey.'

'Towerstack was fit,' I interrupted, 'and right up to the last fence The Reserved Flyer jumped well. I wonder what went wrong at Davidson's end?'

'Don't know, he couldn't have been much more wrong, could he? I'll bet he's not very happy with the people who provide his information. Still, it's not our worry, is it?'

'No, but it could have been. By the way, have you posted the money?'

'Oh yes, first thing we did after collecting the winnings. Arthur took his cut and we stuffed the rest into the envelope and sent it off.'

I arrived back at my so-called flat about an hour later. I picked up a bottle of whisky on the way and another packet of cigarettes. I then spent quite a pleasant evening lying on the bed, drinking, smoking, listening to cassettes, and most of all thinking about Katie.

'Lunch, as far as I am concerned, includes drinks, and as it's my lunch I insist on getting the drinks too. So stop arguing and tell me what you want.' We were sitting in the bar of the recently opened restaurant just around the corner from Arthur's flat, and I was fending off the offers to get the first round. I fended successfully and carried the tray back to the corner where we were sitting. A waiter arrived with five large menus and we sat back to study the delights available.

'Arthur, I haven't brought my glasses with me,' Mrs Clifford said, fiddling in her handbag.

'You don't need your glasses to eat with,' Arthur retorted, without even looking up.

'I know that, but I can't read the menu and that's half the fun. I'll just slip up to the flat and get 'em. I won't be a minute.'

When she'd been gone for about a quarter of an hour, Arthur decided she probably couldn't see her glasses without her glasses. 'I'm sure they're on top of the bleedin' telly,' he swore, turning towards me. 'Do us a favour, lad; nip and tell her.'

'And hurry up, I'm starving,' Jim shouted after me.

The ground floor door of the building was open and I took the stairs two at a time. The door to Arthur's flat was open too, so I gave a polite knock and walked in. 'Arthur says they're on the television, Mrs C.,' I called cheerfully, but to my surprise there was no sign of her. 'Mrs C.,' I shouted, but again no reply. I glanced around the room; it was very much as I remembered from my previous visit. I saw the glasses on the television and next to them lay Arthur's winnings, a big bundle of money held by an elastic band. I made a mental note to reprimand him for leaving it lying about.

'Mrs C.,' I called again. There were two doors leading off the living room. I opened the nearest and looked into a bedroom; it was empty. The other door led to the kitchen; it was slightly ajar so I gave it a push, and found her.

She was lying on the floor with a large, nasty-looking cut on the side of her head, and her face was covered with blood. I dashed into the bedroom, ripped off the bedspread and covered her to keep her warm. Then I ran down the stairs and hammered on the door of the ground-floor flat. It was opened by a middle-aged lady.

'Quickly, there's been an accident upstairs. Phone for an ambulance and then please look after her. I'm going to fetch her husband.' I left the bewildered woman dialling 999 on the payphone in the hall and ran back to the restaurant.

Jim was carrying more drinks to the table as I burst in. My face must have said it all.

'What's the matter?' Sylvia asked, a worried note in her voice.

Arthur looked up, his mouth wide open.

'Your wife's had a fall, Arthur. There's an ambulance on the way.'

He was up out of his seat and running before Jim could put the drinks down. We all followed on. He couldn't run very fast, but he did his best, and we all reached the flat at the same time as the ambulance and police car. The two ambulance men were first in and when we arrived in the living room they were in conference with the lady from downstairs. It turned out she was a Sister from the same hospital and it was she who spoke first.

'Mr Clifford, I'm terribly sorry, but I'm afraid your wife's dead.'

Everyone stood as if in a trance and stared at her for what seemed an eternity, but in fact could only have been a second or two. Sylvia went to put her arm around Arthur's shoulder, but he walked forward, past the Sister, and pushed open the kitchen door. I could see Mrs Clifford's body now totally covered by the bedspread. Arthur knelt beside, drew back the cover and gently stroked his wife's hair.

'Any idea what happened?' Jim asked no one in particular.

'It looks as though she slipped and fell against the cooker; there's blood on it where she hit her head.' The Sister was the one to respond.

'Was there anything I could have done?' I directed my question to one of the ambulance men, but again it was the lady who answered.

'No, she was probably dead when you found her; she probably died instantly. There was nothing anyone could have done.'

The funeral took place the following Wednesday morning. Jim and Sylvia looked after Arthur and made all the arrangements for him. Harry closed the betting shop for the day as a mark of respect and came to the funeral himself. In fact there were only the five of us there: Arthur, Jim, Sylvia, Harry and me.

We stood in the graveyard of a little church and watched in silence as the coffin was lowered slowly into the earth. A light rain blew in our faces and I realised that Arthur was standing with his coat wide open. I leant over and did up one of the buttons. Close to, I could see the drizzle running down his forehead and into his eyes, but he didn't seem to notice. He just looked at the coffin as if to say, 'Whatever will I do without you?'

It was the first time I had been to a funeral. I decided the next one I would go to would be mine.

5

The day after the funeral, Arthur came into work and, remarkably, he sounded much better – he still looked ill – but he seemed better in himself. He brought with him a small present for Jim to give to Sylvia.

'You shouldn't have done, you know,' Jim said.

'It's just a little thank you, that's all. I couldn't have managed these last few days without you and your missus. And that goes for you too, lad,' he added, turning towards me. 'Funny, I was going to give you the letters about the tips, thought you might like them as a sort of memento of our win, but I can't find them.'

'Oh, don't worry about it, Arthur,' I said, unconcerned.

'Funny, I remember putting them in the drawer in the kitchen on Saturday night, but when I went to get them this morning they weren't there. I've looked everywhere but I still can't find 'em.'

I looked at Jim, only to see him staring at me, willing me not to say anything.

'Don't worry, Arthur, it's not important. You probably just moved them. I'll tell you what, shall Jim and I pop back with you tonight and help you have a good look?'

Jim thought it was a good idea, so Arthur agreed.

We spent an hour searching through Arthur's flat, but to no avail; the letters had disappeared without trace. We even checked the dustbins outside, just in case. By the time we finished Arthur looked more than a little weary, and Jim suggested we all go for a quick pint. Understandably the old man declined, saying he would rather be on his own. We made sure he locked the door behind us and then adjourned to the pub.

'Thanks very much,' I said, as Jim placed the two halves of lager onto the soggy beer mats.

He lowered himself into the seat next to mine. 'Well, what do we do now?'

'Let's look at it logically . . .' I paused to gather my thoughts. 'Either Arthur or Mrs Clifford threw the letters away, or somebody took them. Now Arthur says he definitely did not throw them out and, having been through those awful bins, I tend to believe him.'

Jim nodded in agreement. 'I checked around the garden too, just in case they'd blown out of the bin or through the window.'

'So, someone must have taken them . . .' Jim started to say something but I put up my hand to stop him. 'I know what you're going to say, but let me finish.' I took a sip of lager and then began the case for the prosecution. 'Well, I found Mrs C's body, so I could have taken them, but I didn't. The Sister who lives on the ground floor could have, because she was alone in Arthur's flat for at least five minutes, but what possible reason could she have had for taking them? The ambulance men didn't really have the opportunity, and again no motive. So, that just leaves one possibility . . .'

'That somebody broke in, stole the letters and quite probably killed Mrs C. at the same time.' Jim's voice was deadly serious.

'Exactly,' I agreed in a similar tone.

'It's just as well Arthur hasn't arrived at the same conclusion.'

'Yeah, it would probably kill him if he thought something like that had happened. Still, I don't suppose it'll occur to him, certainly not for some time, if ever. After all, losing a few letters becomes pretty insignificant when you've lost your wife.'

We sat quietly for a minute or two. I was thinking what life would be like without Katie, and Jim was probably thinking the same about Sylvia. It was Jim who broke the silence. 'So, as I said a quarter of an hour ago, what do we do now?'

'Well, there's only one person who could have wanted the letters, or even knew they existed for that matter.'

'C. A. Davidson.'

'Right. The guy who wrote them. There was definitely something funny going on with Brass Lock's race, so it stands to reason that he wouldn't want any fishy evidence hanging around, even if he did win a fortune by a fluke.'

'So what do we do?'

'I'll go to the police, but in the meantime you go and see that Sister just in case she did move the letters for some reason.'

'Mr Simms, I think you read too many detective stories . . .'

It was Detective Inspector Lesley who spoke. He was half leaning, half sitting on a small table in one of the interview rooms at the police station. I was perched on the edge of a fairly uncomfortable chair facing him, and had just finished my story for the second time. The only reason the Inspector was there at all was because I had kicked up a fuss, and demanded to see someone important when the desk sergeant refused to take me seriously.

Lesley was a man in his mid-forties, with greying hair and the sort of haggard face that would easily have slotted into his case file of mug shots without detection. He looked as though he had dealt with quite a few cranks in his time, and to him I was probably just another.

'I've heard some tall tales in my time,' he said in disbelief, 'and I like a bet as much as the next man. I just wish someone would send me a few tips like that.'

I started to protest, but Lesley cut me short.

'Mr Simms, I don't know the case at all, so just bear with me for a few minutes while I read the file and talk to the officers involved.' He turned to the policeman standing in the corner of the room. 'Walker is in, isn't he?'

'Yes, sir. He's in the canteen.'

'Get him down to my office and see if you can rustle up a cup of tea for Mr Simms.' They both left, shutting the door behind them. I assumed Walker was the constable who had been at Arthur's flat.

My tea came and I lit a cigarette. In fact I smoked three before they returned. Lesley was carrying a thin file and this time he sat in the chair instead of on the desk.

'Mr Simms, death is a very difficult thing to understand and it becomes even more difficult when it happens to be somebody you know and like very much, particularly when that death arrives in a . . .' Lesley hesitated, searching for the right words, '. . . in an unnatural way. It's difficult to accept, and even in normal circumstances people look for a reason. You have found your reason and by your analysis it is faintly possible that Mrs Clifford was killed. However, let me explain how I know that she was not.' The Detective Inspector was obviously going to 'give evidence' and he carefully placed the emphasis on the right words to make his argument sound plausible. I simply sighed and said nothing.

'Firstly, let us examine the facts, or should I say the fact, because the only thing we know for certain is that Mrs Clifford died after striking her head against the cooker. There is no disputing that. Traces of blood and hair were found on the corner of the stove, the wound corresponds with such an accident, and you yourself said in your statement that she had probably fallen against the cooker.'

He looked at me for approval and reluctantly I nodded my agreement.

'Therefore,' he continued, 'the only thing we have to decide is, did she simply slip, or was she thrown or pushed? Now here, there are a number of factors of which you are probably not aware. Firstly, the living room was a little disarranged and Constable Walker admits there is a vague possibility this could be attributable to a hurried search . . .' I sat up in my seat and looked expectantly at the Inspector, but my hope was in vain. 'But of course, Mr Simms, there was indeed a search going on. Mrs Clifford was looking for her glasses. It was not, as you would have me believe, a horse-race fixer searching for his letters.' He was obviously in full flow, and I could see there would be no point whatsoever in stopping him. 'Now, Mrs Clifford was in a hurry, she didn't want to keep you all waiting in the restaurant, so she was rushing, and there we have my second point. She had removed her shoes at the door, so she would have been in her stockinged feet. The kitchen floor is covered by lino, so it's quite feasible that she slipped, particularly since she would have been concentrating more on finding her glasses than her own safety. Thirdly, the only mark on her body was the wound caused by the fall, and fourthly, there was no indication of a forced entry into the flat. The one last point, perhaps most important of all, was that there was nearly one thousand pounds in cash on top of the television set. Mr Simms, no would-be thief would break into a flat, steal some letters and leave that kind of money lying around.'

'Unless he was disturbed,' I pointed out.

'You're grasping at straws. All you have to go on is a couple of missing letters which the old man probably put in the bin without thinking. You said yourself he's never mentioned any thoughts of anything untoward. So why upset him? Take it from me, Mr Simms, if I felt there was anything sinister going on I would be the first to investigate. The old lady just fell and died; very sad, but it happens every day.'

I stood up and walked towards the door. I didn't say anything. After all, there was very little to say. But as I reached the door the Inspector spoke again.

'By the way, did the race look fixed to you?'

I had to admit that it didn't.

Katie pulled the sheets up around her ears and curled up close. 'But you're still convinced she was killed?'

'I know it's stupid, but yes, I am.'

I had told Katie about the missing letters and my visit to the police station, followed by the quick trip to Jim's just to verify that the Sister in the ground floor flat hadn't seen the letters.

'What did Jim say?' Katie asked.

'He just felt that if the police weren't interested, then that was that, we should leave it there.'

'But you don't think so.' Her voice was full of concern.

'All I know is that I won a lot of money, thanks to Arthur, and the least I can do is try to find out what really happened to his wife. But what I don't want to do is upset him.'

'So don't tell him.'

'No, I don't intend to, at least not until I'm certain, and by then if anything funny did happen it would be common knowledge anyway.'

'Just be careful, that's all. If Mrs Clifford was murdered and someone notices that you're prying . . .' Her voice trailed away; she obviously didn't want to say any more.

I stroked her face gently. 'Don't worry, darling, I'll be careful. And anyway, I don't even know where to start.'

'I do,' she whispered mischievously, as her hand slid back under the covers. 'Why not start at the Co-op?'

The following evening, Harry Greenaway and I sat in the office at the back of the shop. Everybody had gone home and Harry had just poured two coffees. During the day Jim had told him about our concern over Mrs Clifford's death, and he had quietly asked me to stay for a chat after racing was over.

'David, Jim's told me about the letters and the police's view.'

I thought he was about to do an Inspector Lesley on me and tell me to forget it. But I was wrong.

'All I'll say is, be careful,' he continued, 'but if some bastard did do Mrs C. in, then anything I can do to help find him, just ask. Take time off, use the office phone, anything.'

'Thanks, 'Arry. I'll have a go for a week or two, then if nothing turns up I'll forget it. I suppose, when it all boils down, the police could be bloody right.'

'Where are you going to start?'

I was tempted to say at the Co-op, but I didn't fancy having to explain Katie's little 'in' joke, especially since it had all started in Harry's car. So I clamped a smile and discussed what action Harry thought I should take. 'The answer must lie with this Davidson character; he sent Arthur the tips,' I explained.

'But do you know where to find the bugger? Can you remember where Arthur posted his winnings back to?'

'Jim and me were talking about that today. They were all Post Office numbers, but as far as we can remember they were all in different parts of the country.'

'Different parts of the country?'

'I know it looks strange in the light of what's happened, but when some guy's sending you winners like he was, you don't worry too much about the details.'

'I suppose not,' he conceded.

'But I can remember the names of the horses he sent, so I think I'll start there.'

The next day I rang the *Sporting Life* and, posing as a would-be buyer, got the names of the owners and trainers of the five horses in question. Then, after ferreting through back copies of the same paper, I got the names of the jockeys involved. It all proved absolutely useless. There wasn't one common denominator to be found. The only thing the horses had in common was that they were all trained in the North of England, but then the North of England is a bloody big place.

I started by ringing the trainer of Guide, the first horse tipped, and told him I was trying to contact Mr C. A. Davidson and had been

given his number. The trainer said he had never heard of Mr Davidson and, to make matters worse, he sounded completely genuine.

Katie went home for the weekend; I actually suggested going with
her, but she said her mum wasn't very well and the shock of being intro-
duced to a 'private detective' would probably prove too much. So I
woke up Sunday morning with the prospect of spending yet another
Sunday alone. But as it turned out, I was wrong. I was halfway through
listening to my favourite radio programme when there was a knock on
the door.

It was more of a shock than a surprise. During the whole time I had
lived at the flat, I had not had one caller. I sat motionless on the bed,
my skin getting hot and clammy and my mind racing back to the two
strange men on the train. I looked hopefully around the room for a
way out, but I knew the window was my only chance and that was too
far from the pavement to risk it.

A second, louder knock made me jump. I switched off the radio and
cleared my throat in the hope of sounding tough. 'Who is it?' I croaked;
the throat clearing obviously hadn't worked.

'It's me, you silly sod,' came Harry's cheerful reply. 'Come on, I've
been standing here for ages.' I breathed a sigh of relief and let him
in.

'What's the matter?' he asked. 'You look as though you've seen a
ghost.'

'I'm okay. I think being Sherlock Holmes is getting a bit too much
for me. I had visions of two big guys standing outside the door, waiting to tell me with their fists that Mr C. A. Davidson is none of my
business.'

Harry laughed and walked around the room. 'So, this is the David
Simms palace, eh? Well, where's the wonderful coffee you're always
telling me about?'

I moved over to the sink and put the kettle on. 'Famed coffee coming up.' I tipped the ground beans into the filter and waited for the
water to boil.

'Come on then, 'Arry, to what do I owe this honour?' I handed him
the cup and he was kind enough not to check it for cracks.

'Well, on the assumption you still want to be Sherlock Holmes, I
thought you might like to know that Wellington Day is running at
Wolverhampton tomorrow.'

'How interesting, my dear Watson. Do I get the day off?'

'Of course.'

'How do you know it's running?'

'Well, my old television finally gave up last week so I rented a new
one with teletext. The weather's been so bad lately, I thought I'd see

56

if there was any prospect of racing tomorrow, and not only did it say that Wolverhampton was on, it also gave the runners.'

The following morning found me sitting in a train as it was just about to pull out of Euston Station. I was trying desperately to get my breath back, having just run from the underground to the ticket office, then into Menzies to pick up a copy of the *Sporting Life*, and all this within five minutes of the train leaving. It moved out on time too; just as well I hadn't counted on it being late.

I settled back in the seat and put on the earphones of my new personal stereo. I'd brought a couple of tapes for the journey and selected an old Bob Dylan one that I hadn't played for some time. I'd had my new toy for four days now and already I'd learned that only I could hear the music, no one else. That might be an obvious sort of statement to make, but with earphones on you get pretty engrossed in the music, start tapping your feet and bobbing your head to the beat. To gawking onlookers I must have come across as a prospective internee of a mental institution.

Bob Dylan's distinctive voice filled my head as I watched the northern outskirts of London flash quickly by the window. The train wasn't that crowded and I had the two double seats all to myself. Watford came and went, as did Bob Dylan. I decided not to listen to the second side just yet and instead spread my paper out on the table, turning to the page featuring the Wolverhampton card.

Wolverhampton. It seemed strange going back. I hadn't been to the Midlands since my somewhat enforced departure, and in the 'old days' Wolverhampton had been my most frequented racecourse.

Wellington Day was probably the most interesting of all the tips Arthur had received, because it was the one which had been the most heavily backed. It was running in the third race and its easy win last time out had obviously had its effect on the bookmakers. The *Life* estimated that it would start the even-money favourite. I glanced quickly through the other horses in the race and the day suddenly took on a totally different meaning. I leaned back in the seat and laughed. The second favourite in the race was almost as interesting as Wellington Day. I was now looking forward to the afternoon with more than a little excitement.

It was almost like being home again, standing in the grandstand watching the horses canter down for the first race. But I wasn't too concerned with the horses. I was far more interested in the man wearing a grey overcoat and trilby hat, who was just leaving the parade ring and walking towards the stands. He was Tom Martin, the trainer of Wellington Day, and his runner in the first race was just making its way down to the start. There would be five or six minutes before the off so I walked down the steps towards him.

'Excuse me, Mr Martin,' I said politely.

'Yes?' he replied, obviously surprised.

'I'm sorry to bother you, but it's important that I talk to you about Wellington Day's last race.'

Martin looked even more surprised, probably wondering who the hell I was. 'I'm sorry,' he said, 'I can't help you. I didn't train Wellington Day for his last race.'

'Oh,' was all I could say. Some detective, I thought; cocked up the facts at the first try.

A younger man, probably about my age, walked up to the trainer just as I was about to retreat.

'Hello, Tom,' the newcomer said. 'How is he?'

'He's fine. By the way, this gentleman,' Martin gestured towards me, 'was asking questions about Wellington's last race.'

'Was he really?' The younger man spoke slowly, and then turning to me said, 'Perhaps I can help.'

'Yes . . . er . . . but I'm not sure who you are?' There was an obvious hesitation in my voice.

'Likewise,' came the reply.

'Well, my name is David Simms, which probably means nothing to you, but it's very important I speak with someone about Wellington Day's last race.'

'Well, I'm Michael Myers and I own Wellington Day. Now, what is so important about his last race?'

I smiled. There was no hostility in his voice, more a friendly mimicry. He returned my smile, but it turned into a gasp when I told him that I was trying to find the man who had written to Arthur, giving Wellington Day as a certainty.

'What!' he exploded. 'You mean someone wrote to you giving my bloody horse. I think I'd like to talk to you too. Right now!'

The first race had just started, but Michael Myers had no intention of watching it. He grabbed my arm and almost frogmarched me into the members' bar. With the race under way it was virtually empty and we sat at a table by the window.

'I'm sorry,' he said, obviously much calmer now, 'it's just that my horse's last race is rather a sore point with me. Here, let me get you a drink.'

He went to the bar and brought back two whiskies, and I briefly explained the saga of the letters.

'Do you think your friend's wife was murdered?' he asked.

'I don't really know, but I'd like to find out. The police certainly don't.'

The first race finished and the punters were beginning to find their way back into the bar.

'Look,' Michael said, 'we must talk about this in greater detail, but to be honest I'm a bit pushed for time right now and things get hectic, especially if Wellington Day wins.'

'Do you think he will win?' I asked expectantly.

'He should do, easily. There's only one other horse in with a chance, but believe me, Wellington Day is something special. Actually, the reason I'm a bit pushed now is because I've arranged to meet the owner of Wellington's main rival for a drink before the race. But I really would like to discuss this some more. Did you say you live in London?'

'That's right.'

'Well, I'll be in London tomorrow. Could we meet early evening, perhaps?' We agreed on six o'clock in the bar of the Regent Palace Hotel. I was just about to shake his hand and depart when I noticed him look over my shoulder and smile.

'Ah, the opposition has arrived. I'll quickly introduce you and then if you will excuse me . . .'

The room was crowded by now and I had to lean to one side to let him pass. I didn't turn around but I heard him say, 'Hello, glad you could make it. Let me introduce a recent acquaintance of mine, David Simms.'

I turned around and smiled a hello. Elaine Ellerton stood speechless, so I held out my hand. 'Very pleased to meet you.'

I saw her swallow; she struggled to complete the handshake and all she could manage was a very shaky:

'Yes.'

It was definitely exit time so I moved towards the door and waved goodbye to Michael. Outside I leaned against the wall and decided I needed another drink. I went into the public version of the members' bar, ordered a double whisky and wondered what I would have done if it had been George Ellerton standing there instead of Elaine, or even worse, both of them.

The second race finished and I wandered down to the parade ring to have a look at the horses for the most interesting race of the afternoon. However, like the majority of the male punters present, I found myself not taking too much notice of the horses. Instead my gaze was drawn towards the extremely attractive filly standing in the centre of the ring, talking to her trainer.

Elaine looked as lovely as ever; her long blonde hair was tied back with a black bow, revealing facial features that wouldn't have been out of place on the front cover of *Vogue*. Her dress, as usual, was classical and elegant: the long camel coat must have carried a French designer label somewhere and, at five foot eight in her stockinged feet, any designer would have been happy for her to model his creation. It was little wonder the horses had taken a back seat for once.

But Wellington Day looked good, and if Michael Myers was right about his chances, then it would be silly for me not to win a few bob. So I walked down the line of bookies and put on £50 at evens.

Putting that sort of money on a horse would have terrified me a couple of weeks ago. But now, after winning my minor fortune and having a racehorse owner telling me the race was as good as won, I somehow felt differently about the wager. I don't even think I would have minded too much if the horse had lost. But it didn't.

Wellington Day led from start to finish. At the second last hurdle, Ellerton Express looked as though he might make a race of it, but as soon as he got close Wellington Day just pulled clear and won by an easy five lengths.

Not bad, I thought, as I walked back into the members' enclosure. Fifty quid profit should quite easily pay for the day's expenses and leave a tidy margin.

Elaine wasn't difficult to find. She was back in the members' bar sitting in the corner talking to her trainer. I knew he had another horse running in the fifth race and would have to go soon to supervise the saddling, so I stood by the bar and waited. A single whisky later he left and I went over to join my former lover.

'You are rotten,' she said, referring to our meeting earlier that afternoon.

'Sorry, but I couldn't resist it,' I laughed.

'What on earth are you doing here?'

I decided not to tell her about the letters. 'Well, when I noticed your horse was running, I thought I would come and see it.'

She took a packet of cigarettes out of her handbag and offered me one.

'I've only just started again,' I admitted, taking one from the opened packet, an element of resignation in my voice. I could feel my eyes involuntarily searching the bar. Elaine must have noticed.

'It's all right,' she said, 'he's not here, he never comes to the races. He's never had any interest in it, and I don't think he's about to start just because I've . . .' she paused, '. . . I should say, the company's got a racehorse.'

'Then why did he buy it?' I asked, slightly puzzled.

'Because I wanted one. After the er . . . accident,' she looked up at me as if wondering if that was the right word to use, 'or at least after George's initial fury had subsided, I think he was actually worried about losing me, so whatever I mentioned he bought, and a racehorse was one of the first things.'

Out of the corner of my eye I noticed a man walking towards us.

'Your horse ran a good race, Mrs Ellerton,' he said casually.

'Oh y-yes, thank you,' Elaine stammered. The man nodded towards me out of politeness and walked out of the bar. Elaine could sense my own unease. 'I think he was one of the other owners in my race,' she said, by way of explanation.

I finished my whisky with a single gulp and, having regained my composure, remembered my manners. 'I'm sorry, I should have offered you a drink.'

'No thanks, I don't think sitting here and talking to you is doing my nerves any good either. Not that anyone would think it unusual seeing me in general conversation on a racecourse.'

'It's okay,' I interrupted, 'I know what you mean.'

'But I would like to talk to you, just to hear what you've been doing. I felt very guilty about you losing your job. How did you get here?'

'On the train.'

'Well, let me give you a lift back to the station.'

The next race had just started, so there were very few people about as we walked out of the track and into the parking area reserved for the élite of the sport. Elaine stopped by a silver Mercedes and took the keys from her handbag.

'Where's the BMW?' I asked, surprised.

'That went with the accident. I've got a Porsche now, but this is George's.' She threw her coat into the back as I sank into the passenger seat and smiled at the thought of what George would say if he knew his wife was giving me a lift in his car. I took out my cigarettes and passed one to Elaine, lighting them both with the car lighter as we glided out of the parking area. I opened the ashtray, but it was stuffed full of brightly coloured sweet papers. I looked across at Elaine.

'You'll never keep that beautiful figure if you eat like this,' I joked.

She glanced across at the ashtray. 'That's nothing to do with me,' she said disapprovingly.

Sitting so close, I had an incredible urge to touch her, so I put my hands in my pockets. Physically she was irresistible.

The traffic was fairly light as we drove towards the city. We must have driven that way many times before, but now it all seemed years ago – except for Elaine, she still looked just as I remembered. I wondered if she was worth all the problems she had caused me. I tried to convince myself that she wasn't, but the more I looked at her . . . I needed to change my train of thought so I pressed the play button on the cassette player built neatly into the dashboard. Music always helped, soothed the carnal thoughts.

The stereo speakers eased into life and filled the car with the less than appropriate words of Barbra Streisand asking, 'If we had the chance to do it all again, would we? Could we?' I pushed the stop button with a little too much force and the cassette leapt out onto the floor.

'Funny, I was just thinking the same,' my beautiful chauffeuse said.

I couldn't help it, I had to ask the question. 'Well, would you?'

Some traffic lights turned red; she stopped the car and turned to look at me. 'David,' she said seriously, 'I wanted to run away with you so many times . . .' The lights changed without us noticing and the car behind gave a polite hoot on the horn.

'Then why didn't you?' I asked, as we started moving again.

'Well, firstly, you never asked, and secondly, I think we would have been broke.'

'I can certainly confirm the second point,' I said with conviction.

Elaine pulled into a multi-storey car park at the back of the Manders Shopping Centre, and I told her about the problems I'd had getting a job, and how I eventually ended up working in the bookies for Harry. To say she was surprised was an understatement. She couldn't imagine George going to such lengths to quash any job opportunities I might have had, particularly since he had never so much as mentioned my name since the 'event'. 'Then again, he is such a vindictive sod, I suppose it shouldn't come as a total shock. But I would have thought you could get a proper job now. After all, it's so long ago.'

'I probably could, but for the time being I quite like working at the bookies.'

'I bet you gamble away all your pay,' she teased.

'No, I'm very good about it.' I didn't explain that it was a question of survival first, and that after eating there was little left. I felt it was time to change the subject. 'That's enough about me, let's talk about you.'

'Not much to tell really. After our accident I thought George would throw me out, but he went totally the other way. When I think about it, throwing me out would have been as good as admitting I'd had an affair, and I don't think his ego could have stood that. So instead, he seemed to make a conscious effort to keep me.'

'So he bought you the horse.'

'He said it was tax deductible as long as it ran under the company's name, but to all intents and purposes, I suppose it's mine.'

'Do you get much information from your trainer?'

'Looking for tips?' The smile on her face said she took the question in the nicest possible way.

'No, just interested really.' I tried to sound casual. 'I just wondered if being in the racing business made much difference. I mean, you read about betting coups all the time, and the information must come from the inside, the trainers initially.'

'When Ellerton Express first ran, my trainer thought he might win, but he had no way of assessing the opposition. Today, again, he thought the horse could win, but didn't really know how good Wellington Day would be. So he was right once, and wrong once, if you want to look at it that way. But I would never have said the information was a tip, more the trainer's professional opinion.'

'What about your trainer's other horses, or those in nearby stables?' Again, I tried to sound as if I was asking simply out of interest.

'He obviously must know when his other horses have a good chance, and occasionally when I go to the stables he may talk about them, but I never hear anything about other stables. But he knows I don't gamble, so perhaps he never bothers to tell me anything.'

I looked at my watch: it was make your mind up time. Did I go for my train, or stay a little longer with Elaine? As it happened, the decision wasn't mine. Elaine had noticed the glance at my wrist.

'Yes, I must go too,' she said. 'I'll drive you to the station.'

'Don't worry, it's probably quicker if I walk. The traffic will be heavy by now.' I reached over and squeezed her hand. 'It's been lovely seeing you again,' I said, and kissed her on the cheek. Quickly I opened the door and jumped out. Walking around in front of the car, I heard the electric window go down.

'David!' There was almost a touch of desperation in her voice, and I stopped in my tracks. If it had been a film I would have walked out of the car park without even looking back. But it wasn't a film and I was never a good actor. I went back to the open window, leaned inside and kissed her again, but this time not on the cheek. She held me for a moment and then whispered urgently, 'I will see you again, won't I?'

'I expect so,' I nodded.

'You can always find me, any time Ellerton Express is running. I'll always be there on my own.'

I wondered if everyone else experienced the same problem. Just how the hell do you get out of Piccadilly tube station at the right exit? There just seemed to be so many of them and, true to form, I emerged into the cold evening air on the wrong side of the street. I looked across in the direction of the Regent Palace Hotel and, sure enough, there was the tube sign right by it. My eyes wandered momentarily back down the length of stairs I had just climbed. Damn it, I thought, I'm not going back into the same maze; I'll probably end up in Leicester Square! So, taking my life in my hands, or should I say my feet, as soon as the traffic lights changed to red, I made a dash across the road. Halfway over, the lights in another direction moved to green and drivers, who obviously thought they were at Le Mans, started to bear down on me. Nought to sixty in six seconds had nothing on me; I dropped down a gear and, with adrenalin flowing, was on the other pavement just in time to feel the air from their slipstream. I stopped briefly to catch my breath and wave them on with my handkerchief.

One thing about London, compared to other cities in the country, was that there always seemed to be plenty going on. Even though it was seven in the evening and a fairly wet evening at that, most of the shops were still open and, as I walked past a crowded Wimpy Bar towards the main entrance of the hotel, I wondered briefly where all the people would go when the evening was over. Who would they go back to? Were they happy?

I certainly felt happy. Confused, but happy. The previous day's journey back from Wolverhampton had seemed to take no time at all. I hadn't listened to any cassettes or even glanced at the evening newspaper. Strange to think I once worked for that same newspaper. I just sat on the train, then the tube, and finally walked back to my flat, deep in thought, memories of a past existence: Elaine, Wolverhampton, the races; it had all come flooding back.

But I'd been brought back to reality with a jolt when I walked into my flat to find Katie sitting there listening to one of my tapes. I realised with a sense of guilt that I hadn't given her a thought for most of the day, which seemed rather strange, particularly since I had spent the last however many days thinking about almost nothing else. Still, seeing her sitting there waiting for me brought back all the feelings temporarily pushed to one side. We went to bed and I told her how much I loved her. When she asked about my day, I explained about winning the fifty quid and also about my arrangement to meet Michael Myers. I didn't tell her about Elaine, or even about Elaine's horse. I thought it better not to.

So there I sat in the bar of the Regent Palace Hotel, waiting for Michael Myers to arrive. I wasn't sure what good it would do talking to him, maybe no good at all, but at the same time I didn't know what good friends we were to become. At that time I didn't know a lot of things.

I was just ordering a whisky when he walked in. The room was fairly empty, so he had no difficulty in recognising me. We shook hands; he had a strong grip and a smile which looked as though he was genuinely pleased to see me.

'What can I get you to drink, Michael?' I automatically thought of him as Michael. He tried to pay, but I insisted, pointing out that I had won a few bob on his horse the day before. He said he would buy the next round, and we moved into a corner seat so that we could talk with a little more privacy.

Michael Myers was about my age, but that's where the similarity ended.

He was perhaps two inches taller, with fair hair and a light moustache. I was glad I had decided to wear one of my good suits because he was smartly dressed in a tweed sports jacket, open-necked shirt and light-coloured trousers.

Since I had made the initial approach, I thought it only fair to tell him as much as possible, so I started with Arthur's first letter and worked my way through. I was careful not to go into any of my previous background and I kept it strictly 'business', not mentioning Katie, and especially steering well away from Elaine. Throughout my story Michael sat quietly, slowly slipping his whisky. At the point where I found Arthur's wife, he was about to say something, but then changed his mind. When I eventually stopped talking, he walked to the bar and bought two more drinks. He put the whiskies on the small table and sat back.

'That's absolutely amazing,' he said. I must have looked slightly offended because he quickly tried to qualify his statement. 'When I say amazing, I mean . . . amazing!' He was obviously shocked and had great difficulty in finding a more suitable word to express himself. 'It's not that I don't believe you,' he continued, 'it's just that the whole thing is . . . is . . .'

'Amazing?' I suggested light-heartedly.

We both laughed and Michael asked how I thought he could help. I had to confess that I didn't really have a clue.

'But you must have had some idea when you came to see me at Wolverhampton,' he pressed.

'I suppose I hoped that you would know this Davidson character, or at least have an idea who would have passed on information about your horse's apparent ability to win his first hurdle race with ease.'

'And who the bastard was who had all the money on it,' he said, with obvious feeling.

Now it was my turn to be amazed. 'It wasn't you then?'

He shook his head. 'Okay, so you've told me your story. I think I had better tell you mine, although it's certainly not as exciting . . . or as sad,' he added quietly.

It turned out that Michael Myers was a singer, or to be more exact, a pianist first and a singer second. He was two years younger than me and lived alone in a flat in Stockport. His flat sounded a bit better than mine, but then that wouldn't be difficult. He explained that he had been professional for almost three years, and prior to that had been teaching music in one of the large comprehensive schools just outside Stockport. He had always wanted to play the piano for a living but hadn't the courage to give up his teaching job – well, at least not until his wife ran away with the English teacher.

'Dennis and I were quite good friends – Dennis was the English teacher,' Michael pointed out, 'so to come home one day and find a note from my wife saying she'd gone off with him came as quite a blow.'

There wasn't anything I could do but agree.

'But I guess it was the push I needed. A couple of days later, after a particularly bad afternoon with the brats in school, I drove into Manchester, walked into an agent's office and told the guy I could play the piano and sing a bit. I don't really know what I expected, but I certainly didn't expect him to send me straight around to a club to play that evening. Apparently the regular pianist had gone sick and the agent was just about to start ringing around for a stand-in. I became the stand-in. I didn't know what sort of music to play, whether I needed to speak or anything, but the guy who ran the club told me it wouldn't matter what I did because no bugger would listen anyway – they'd all be too busy eating, getting pissed, or chatting up the birds.'

I laughed, but at the same time found myself wondering why he was telling me all this. Not that I minded, because I found Michael intriguing. He must have sensed my curiosity because he suddenly broke off from his autobiography.

'I hope I'm not boring you,' he said, 'but there is a reason for the general story. Although, I must admit, I didn't intend going into such detail.'

I urged him to continue.

'Well, I made the buggers listen,' he said with a broad grin, 'and the little guy who ran the place told me to come back the following night. That was all the encouragement I needed. The next day I rang the school and politely told the deputy head where he and the little brats could stick the job, and ever since then I've been playing in various clubs, restaurants and hotels all over the North of England.'

'What sort of music do you play?'

'Almost anything. I trained to be a classical pianist, but I tend to play the more well-known popular tunes; it depends what the audience wants. Do you like music?'

'Addicted to it,' I admitted, 'but mostly sixties or seventies.'

'Oh, I can do all that, Elton John and the Beatles to flower-power and jive. Why don't you come and listen to me tonight?'

'Where are you playing?'

'Garry's. It's a new night club just off St James's Square. I'm playing in the bar. Apparently it's very exclusive but I'm sure I could arrange for you to get in.'

'I'd like that very much. Do you think I could bring someone with me?' I asked hopefully.

'I don't see why not. I'll fix it with the guy on the door. Is she nice?' he asked with a grin.

The bar was starting to fill up, so I took the opportunity to attract the barmaid's attention and order two more drinks. I also bought a new packet of cigarettes. Michael said he didn't smoke, but that didn't stop me lighting one.

'Anyway,' my musical companion continued, 'let me finish telling you why your story interested me so much. Being a musician certainly pays better than being a teacher, but it doesn't make me a wealthy man by any stretch of the imagination, and it definitely does not pay enough to keep a racehorse in training. Unfortunately, I didn't actually realise that until after I'd bought Wellington Day. I'd always been a keen racegoer and I've backed horses since I was fifteen, but never heavily. In fact, if I put a fiver on a horse it was a very big occasion.'

'Likewise,' I admitted.

'Anyway, one day I went to Carlisle races with a friend of mine who's a vet. Wellington Day ran in the second race and, as usual in his flat racing days, he finished well down the field. We'd both backed him, mainly because of his breeding, but also because he'd finished third in his last race and we thought he might at last show the promise his breeding suggested. But as I said, he ran his usual disappointing race and it was purely by chance we later found ourselves in the members' bar talking to the horse's owner. Actually it was the owner's racing manager we were talking to, because at that time Wellington Day was owned by one of the Arab Sheikhs on the racing scene. My veterinary friend asked if he intended sending the horse hurdling, but the illustrious racing manager explained the horse's trouble was that he was far more interested in mares than in racing, and the only place he was likely to send him was the knacker's yard, that is if he didn't sell him at the sales.'

'Were you actually interested in buying, then?'

'At that moment I had no intention whatsoever of buying Wellington Day, or any other horse for that matter, but I asked purely out of interest how much he'd expect the horse to fetch at the sales. The Sheikh's man must have thought I was keen on buying, so he said if I was interested I could have him there and then for eight hundred guineas. He pointed out that I'd be getting a bargain because the Sheikh had paid over a hundred times more than that for the horse as a yearling. I was just about to back off by saying the nag was useless, when to my amazement my friend grabbed my arm and told me to buy it, and in a moment of madness I did.

'Afterwards I asked my veterinary surgeon, as he had now become, what had possessed him to suggest that I buy the horse, and worse still, why he had let me go through with it. Simple, he'd said, Wellington Day might turn out to be a good horse.'

And Wellington Day had turned out to be an exceptional horse. The transformation had occurred when Michael, at the vet's suggestion, had him gelded. It had the desired effect of turning him off the female version of the species for good. It also caused the horse to grow quite quickly – again something the friendly vet had predicted.

'But if just having his whatsits chopped off made so much difference,' I asked, 'then why didn't the Sheikh get it done?'

'Bit painful for him, I think,' Michael laughed.

'I did mean the horse, Michael.'

'I know,' he laughed again, 'but seriously, I thought the same at the time, but if you were an Arab Sheikh with hundreds of horses and millions of pounds, I doubt if you would have time to bother about one horse that on the face of it wasn't that good.'

I nodded in agreement.

'To be honest,' Michael went on, 'I don't think it was just the gelding which caused Wellington's transformation. As soon as he saw a hurdle he simply flew over it, and he's loved jumping ever since.'

'So you picked up a hurdling superstar for a mere eight hundred?'

'Yes, but even when I started having him trained over the hurdles, I thought I had made a financially disastrous mistake.'

I looked at him quizzically.

'Have you any idea how much it costs to keep a racehorse?' he continued.

I had to admit I didn't.

'Well, having found a trainer willing to train him, that was Neil Lancaster, and then having paid a small fortune to get the horse to his stables, I started paying out for registrations at Weatherbys, buying my racing colours, blacksmith's fees, schooling fees . . . and have you any idea how much a horse eats?'

I shook my head again, realising that, for someone who worked in a bookies, I was pretty ignorant about racing matters.

'Anyway, if it hadn't been for my personal vet doing his bit very much on the cheap, I would probably have given up. In fact, after the horse had been in training for a couple of months and Neil Lancaster pronounced him fit and good enough to win his opening race, I was virtually broke. All I had left out of the money saved from my club appearances was a thousand pounds, which I kept out of reach in a building society for a rainy day. The rainy day, I decided, would be Wellington's first race. My trainer thought he would start at about five or six to one, and he was absolutely convinced he'd win. I was fairly honest about my financial state and told him I was going to put the whole thousand on, and it was actually Neil Lancaster who suggested I spread it around to keep the starting price up. So I spent the whole morning driving around getting five hundred on in twenties and thirties, and the vet put the other five hundred on for me in bits in London. It meant that, when I was on the racecourse, I didn't actually have to put a bet on. Lancaster told me he'd put on a couple of hundred himself, but since he was the trainer and trainers often backed their own horses, it wouldn't affect the starting price.

'I noticed the prices on offer with the various bookies as I was walking down to the parade ring, and Wellington seemed to be around the five to one mark. I didn't take any notice after that because I was too much on edge. Just standing in the parade ring was a fantastic thrill, and the walk back up to the stands seems a daze now. Well, as you know, Wellington won by miles and still it didn't occur to me to check the starting price. In fact, it wasn't until I was driving back into Peterborough that I heard it on the radio. Seven to four. I just couldn't believe it. I should have won around five thousand, but ended up with less than two. I thought it was my trainer cocking up the price, and in a fit of temper lasting most of the following week, I swapped stables.'

The bar was quite crowded by now. I had gone through three cigarettes listening to Michael talk, and decided I was smoking far too much. That didn't stop me lighting another.

'Was it Neil Lancaster who backed it then?' I quizzed.

'He swore it wasn't, and quite honestly I tend to believe him now, although I didn't at the time.'

'So who did back it?'

'No idea. Once I realised just how good Wellington was, I wasn't too bothered . . .' he paused, '. . . but I am now.'

'Are you sure we can get in here?'

The club looked expensive and I had to confess that, like Katie, I had my reservations. But I was wearing one of the good suits and Katie looked sensational in a black evening number she'd never had opportunity to wear before. We took a deep breath and marched up to the commissionaire, but we needn't have had any reservations – we actually had a reservation! A table for two, complete with candle and champagne, courtesy of the pianist.

We danced, drank and hummed along to Michael's playing. By two in the morning, during a slow romantic smooch, we decided it was time to leave. We said goodbye to Michael and caught a taxi back to the flat.

'What are you thinking?' Katie asked, propping herself up on one elbow so she could see my face.

I was staring straight up at the ceiling, and had been since we made love. I pulled the sheet over her shoulders in an attempt to keep her warm. 'What to do next, I suppose.'

During the evening I had explained to Katie what Michael had told me, and I had also made arrangements to meet him at his hotel the following day to plan our next move. Our next move? I wondered, was he really interested? He was a successful musician with a horse worth a small fortune. Why should he be bothered with me and my quest?

'What do you think, darling?' I gently pulled Katie down onto my shoulder.

'I don't know what to think. I don't like you playing detective, you might get hurt, and what happens if in the end Arthur's wife actually did slip? It would be such a waste of time and a lot of heartache.'

We were both very tired and I thought it better not to tell Katie what I had decided to do, at least for the time being anyway.

The following evening, when I arrived back in the flat, Katie was already there. She was trying to tidy the place up a bit, but with little success. 'Fancy a weekend in Yorkshire?' I asked.

Even with all the business travel when I worked at Ellerton Press, I had never been to Yorkshire before.

The place where Wellington Day had been trained for his first win was a little village about thirty miles north of Harrogate. Harry let me borrow his car and, since he knew a little bit about the area, courtesy of his sister, he suggested that Harrogate was a nice place to stay. So Katie and I took his advice and booked into a fairly good hotel on one of their cheap weekend packages.

On the journey up, I told Katie that I really had no idea what I was looking for, but hoped that if I could talk to some of the locals, or even better, the stable lads, then I might get some information on the elusive Mr Davidson.

Katie suggested that we take a drive out to the village in the daylight first. That way we could get our bearings and return in the evening, on the assumption that the stable lads would like a drink on a Saturday night and might be a little more willing to talk.

Not only was it a good idea, but it was also the first positive step Katie had taken in my 'investigations'. Strangely enough, I didn't like it. If I was going to run into any trouble, I certainly didn't want Katie around; I just couldn't bear the thought of anything happening to her.

We checked into our hotel at around eleven on the Saturday morning. Katie took one look at the shops and instantly regretted her earlier suggestion, although soon changed her mind as we drove northwards into the Dales.

The village was an hour's drive away and turned out to be a quaint, attractive little place, made even better by the sun shining. We parked in the car park, or rather a cobbled area used for parking, right in the middle of the village. It was centred with a large stone cross and on either side were cafés, pubs and the occasional grocery-type shop for the locals. The village was obviously geared for tourism in the summer, but in early December, even at two in the afternoon, the place was almost deserted.

We wandered into one of the pubs and asked quite an attractive look-ing barmaid if we were too late to get something to eat. Since we were virtually the only people in the pub, getting food did not prove diffi-cult. Even better, the girl was a mine of information.

It turned out there were no less than twelve racehorse trainers in the area, and true enough most of the lads would be in the pubs that night. On the way out I tried a long shot and asked if she knew an acquain-tance of mine, a Mr C. A. Davidson. She thought for a few moments and then shook her head, saying the name didn't ring a bell.

Back in Harrogate, we had afternoon tea in a superb café. We ate scones and enormous cream cakes in a window-seat overlooking gar-dens and parkland. It made it seem more of a holiday and, more importantly, it saved me the trail around the shops, clinging onto Katie's coat tails.

As tea drew to a close, I pointed out that we had the novelty of a warm room just up the road. Katie needed no encouragement and we dashed back to the luxurious freedom of making love on top of the bed, rather than huddled beneath a ton of sheets.

I decided to go sleuthing in the village pubs at around nine-thirty, by which time I reckoned most of the lads would be well oiled and fair-ly chatty. I had great difficulty in persuading Katie to stay back at the hotel, but I just didn't feel happy about her joining me. I eventually managed it by convincing her that it would be easier for me to get infor-mation without a female presence.

So, at about half past eight, with Katie in bed watching television, I got behind the steering wheel and started my first serious bit of 'Sher-lock Holmesing'. Being a naïve sort of private investigator, I assumed a bunch of drunken stable lads would love to chat about Wellington Day, especially if I bought a round or two. It's surprising how wrong you can be.

However, the evening took a strange turn before I even got to speak to a stable lad. By my reckoning I was still a quarter-of-an-hour's drive from the village. It had started to rain and I was taking it fairly care-fully down the narrow roads when my headlights picked out a figure walking along the grass verge. As I got closer I could see it was a woman, and she was walking in the same direction as I was travelling. As far as I could remember, there were no houses between there and the vil-lage, so it was reasonable to assume she and I were heading for the same place. A fine piece of deduction, eh Watson!

I slowed down and pulled up just in front of her. I leaned over and wound down the passenger window. 'Need a lift?' I asked as pleasant-ly as I could, but she totally ignored me and carried on walking. She looked like a drowned rat, hardly surprising since it was raining heav-ily, but what did surprise me was that I recognised her. I put the car into gear and moved forward. Her step quickened, probably from panic; girls walking down lonely country lanes at night don't need male motorists pestering them. I pulled the car slightly past her but this time I got out, leaving the door open so there was at least some light. I spoke to her from my side of the car.

'You're the girl from the pub; you served my girlfriend and me this lunchtime, remember?' I hoped that bringing Katie into the conversation might help. This time she stopped, but still didn't seem too confident. 'Look,' I said, as reassuringly as possible, 'you obviously need a lift, you're soaking wet and a good hour's walk from home, so . . .' I tried to sound a bit more commanding, '. . . get into the car, or we're both going to be soaked stood here.'

There was a moment's hesitation, then she reached down and opened the door. I got in my side, fastened my seatbelt and pulled away.

'Thanks very much.' It was the first time she had spoken.

'Shouldn't you be at work?' I asked, trying to make light of the situation.

'I only work lunchtimes,' she answered, not appreciating my humour.

Her hair was dripping and I apologised for not having anything for her to dry it with.

Having recovered some of her composure, she told me that, against her better judgement, she had gone out to dinner with a man who had been pestering her for a date. After the meal, he stopped the car in a quiet lane and, when she refused his advances, he made her get out until she changed her mind. She obviously hadn't changed her mind and that was where I came in.

'What a bastard,' I said.

'The world is full of them,' was her cynical reply.

'I know, I'm looking for one.'

'The man you asked me about today?'

'That's right, Mr C. A. Davidson. Have you really never heard of him?' I felt it was worthwhile pressing the matter.

She thought for a moment. 'No, honestly, I'd tell you if I had.'

'Does a horse called Wellington Day mean anything to you?'

'I don't know much about the horses, but it rings a bell.' Then it must suddenly have occurred to her that I was alone. 'Where's your girlfriend?' The worried tone had crept back into her voice.

'Back at the hotel in Harrogate.'

'Then what are you doing here?'

I wasn't sure what or how much to tell her, but having a local who was by now glad I had given her a lift was too good an opportunity to miss. 'I'm trying to find out who would have known that Wellington Day was certain to win a race at Huntingdon about two months ago and would have told this Davidson guy.'

'Are you the police or the newspapers?'

'Neither. Funnily enough I work for a bookie, but that's got nothing whatsoever to do with it. I was hoping I could chat to a few drunken stable lads and get some answers.'

'You'll be wasting your time. Nobody – stable lads, trainers, or anyone – will give you any information about anything. They're used to punters trying to pick up tips. The lads will be quite happy for you to buy them drinks, but they won't give anything away.'

By now we were pulling into the village, so I had one more try. 'But I'm not after tips, just how one particular tip came about and who was involved at the receiving end.'

She was halfway out of the car when she turned and spoke in a deadly serious tone. 'Look, be careful. People don't like strangers asking questions. You won't learn anything, so why not go back to your girlfriend and have a nice quiet weekend. Thanks for your help.' With that, she closed the door and was gone.

There had been nothing sinister in what she had said. It seemed to me she was just trying to say: don't meddle in a world full of meddlers, particularly when those within the sport didn't think too highly of such folk.

I parked the car by the stone cross and walked to the nearest pub. I had imagined it to be heaving with eighteen- or nineteen-year-old lads, all chatting away about what was going to win next week. It wasn't. The bar was less than half full, with the majority of people sitting in smallish groups around tables, just talking quietly, or playing dominoes or darts. It certainly was not what I had expected; I could have been in a pub in Earls Court! Also, the stable lads were not all lads. Many of them were stable men, and some stable old men, even a few stable women.

I ordered half a lager and stood by the bar. Ten minutes passed and I hadn't spoken to a soul; getting into conversation with one of the groups looked like being an impossibility. But I did have one small thing going for me, because where I was standing turned out to be on the way out to the gents, and eventually one of the darts players announced, seemingly to the world, that he was going for a pee and brushed past me. He was slightly smaller than me, but stockily built; I guessed he was in his mid-thirties. I didn't know if he had anything to do with horses, but it was going to be my best chance so far, so I decided to go for the bull, so to speak.

Two minutes later, as he was walking back towards me, I turned slightly as he was about to pass. 'Excuse me.'

He seemed amazed that I had ventured to speak to him. His lips didn't move, but his face had a questioning look about it, so I continued. 'You don't know if Mr Davidson will be in tonight, do you?'

'No idea, mate.' With that, he walked back to his darts. The answer was given in such a way to suggest that, not only had he no idea who I was talking about, but also that he couldn't care less. Still, I drew some encouragement from the incident – at least I had spoken to somebody and it just might have got me into conversation, so I moved to another pub and tried again.

In the third pub it worked. There were two men, both in their early twenties, standing at the bar and actually talking about the day's racing. I bought my third lager of the evening and gently interrupted their conversation.

'Excuse me, you don't happen to know if Mr Davidson will be in this evening, do you?'

'Who?' replied the one furthest away.

'Davidson. Mr C. A. Davidson.'

'What's 'e look like?' the other one chipped in.

Now, there was a question. If I knew what he looked like I wouldn't be here, but did I dare admit to not knowing anything about him? I decided that semi-honesty was the best policy.

'Well, to be frank with you, I've never met the guy. You see, he's a professional gambler and occasionally I put bets on for him. He usually just writes to me with the name of the horse and the stake money, only earlier this week he wrote asking me to meet him this evening in a pub here.' I felt quite pleased with myself; they both appeared to believe me and I was now in conversation with them. They were both around my height, one with fairly scruffy brown hair, the other marginally smarter with a moustache. Both were getting low on their drinks, so I arranged for two new pints.

'These horses, do they win?' the moustached one asked.

'Most do; not all, mind you.'

'Lucky you. We work in the stables here and we don't know what's gonna win most of the bleedin' time.'

'Actually, a couple of the horses he's sent have come from up this way, Guide and Wellington Day.' I felt it was time to open things up a bit, see if I could get a reaction. 'This Davidson guy said that Wellington Day was a real good thing, and it was too, won by miles. Having said that, it was backed heavily.'

'Wellington Day ain't trained up 'ere any more,' the long-haired one said.

A breakthrough! 'Was he in your stables?'

'No,' came the short, sharp answer.

So I tried again. 'Out of interest, would you have known if . . .' I tried to make it sound casual, '. . . Wellington Day was going to win?'

'Well, you get rumours, but if you believed everything you hear, you'd be bleeding' broke.'

I didn't really believe him, so I kept plugging away. 'Well, my Davidson character obviously knew it was a cert, so somebody must have told him.'

I didn't get an answer, as a group of men came into the bar and, with a quick 'thanks for the drinks', my two went over to join them. I finished my half and moved on to the fourth pub. As far as I could see, it was the last one in the village.

Here, I did better again. This time I spoke to three separate groups. In each case I had virtually the same conversation, using Wellington Day as my example, and each time I got the same answer – nothing. It was getting towards closing time and, since I was getting nowhere fast, the thought of Katie back at the hotel suddenly took on immense appeal. I felt slightly despondent about my investigative failure and decided on the more direct approach the following day, with visits to both Wellington Day's ex-trainer and Guide's stable.

I left the pub and started my walk over the cobblestones uphill towards the car. It was dark, drizzly and very cold. As I glanced around to check I'd visited every pub in sight, I thought I saw something move in the shadows to my left. Instinctively I hesitated and sure enough a boy – well, sixteen or seventeen – appeared out of the darkness.

'Oy, Mister. Hear you're interested in Wellington Day?' His voice was little above a whisper.

'Yes, that's right, I am,' I said, the excitement rising.

'Come 'ere, I can't be seen talking to ya in the street.' He disappeared into an alleyway, and like a mug I followed.

My eyes had difficulty in adjusting to the dark, but I appeared to be going behind one of the pubs. The boy stopped, and I was about to ask him what he knew when somebody grabbed me from behind and two other men appeared at the front of me. I struggled to free myself, but the arms held me like a vice. Obviously restraining me was a damn sight easier than restraining horses.

One of the men moved forward and brought his fist hard into my stomach. I let out a cry of pain and tried to double up, but the vice held me firm.

'Interested in horses, are we?' my assailant's voice said menacingly. 'Well, let me give you a tip.' Each time he paused, his fist thudded into my body. 'Keep your effin' nose . . .' thump, '. . . out of business that doesn't concern you . . .' thump, '. . . otherwise you'll get hurt . . .' thump, '. . . just like you're going to be now.'

I felt desperately weak and wanted to be sick. I hadn't been in a fight since I was at school, but you don't get brought up on a rough council estate without a little knowledge of the art of survival. The other two seemed to be moving in for the proverbial kill, so I lifted my right leg and brought it down as hard as I could on my restrainer's foot. He let out a gasp and his grip relaxed for a second. I shoved my right elbow back into his ribs with all the power I could muster. His grip broke and he staggered back against the wall. I tried to make a break for it, but only succeeded in crashing into a dustbin. The bin went one way, the lid the other, and I ended up on the floor. There was no time to recover the situation, as all four of them started to prove they were footballers as well as boxers.

Strangely enough, the bin which foiled my escape turned out to be the reason for me not being kicked to a pulp. As I fell, it made such a din that a light went on at the other side of the wall and a voice asked who was there. My assailants changed sports to Olympic sprinters and left.

A door in the wall opened and a shaft of yellow light fell across the alleyway. I must have looked horrific lying amidst the rubbish, groaning, and sure enough there was a gasp as she saw me.

'Can you get up?' She offered me her hand. At the third attempt I managed it, but had to lean against the wall for support.

'Why didn't you just go, like I told you to?' My head stopped spinning and I realised it was the girl from the pub, the one I had picked up in the rain earlier.

'Just persistent, I guess.' I cleared my throat. 'It means a lot to me.'

'You . . .' She started to say something, then changed her mind.

'Thanks for saving me,' I said, and began to walk very slowly towards the main street.

She moved through the door, half closed it, then said, 'Please don't come back. You were kind to me earlier and I wouldn't like to see you hurt . . . and anyway, the man you want isn't here.'

I stopped and looked at her expectantly.

'Try Frankie Allen,' she whispered, 'but please, I never told you that.' She shut the door and I heard the bolt slide across.

The drive back to Harrogate seemed to take an age. I ached from top to toe, my head was splitting and I dreaded to think what I looked like. Fortunately I was able to park right outside the front door of the hotel. I waited until I saw the receptionist leave the front desk, then I made a dash through the door and into the lift. Running nearly killed me, but it was easier than trying to explain why I looked like I did. There was a mirror in the lift and the strip lighting did little for my appearance. My face was splattered with blood from a cut above my right eye, but you couldn't actually see the cut because it was camouflaged with mud. My coat was caked and one of the sleeves was hanging on by a thread.

Katie was sitting up in bed reading a magazine when I walked in. After the initial hysterics, the 'I told you so's' and the 'is there anything broken?', I got into a hot bath and just lay there whilst Katie went to get me a large, a very large, whisky.

76

Later, I told her what I had found out and naturally she asked the inevitable question: 'Who is Frankie Allen?'

I gave the inevitable answer: 'I haven't got a clue.'

6

The following day I asked Katie if she would mind going back to London on the train, since I had decided to go over to Stockport to see Michael. Although she was disappointed at not being able to spend more time with me, after the shock of the previous night I guessed she wasn't too unhappy to be leaving Yorkshire.

I telephoned Michael and said to expect me early afternoon, but I was careful not to mention anything of the previous night's adventure. He sounded quite pleased at the prospect of my visit, saying he was playing at a club in Manchester that night so he would take me along. I wondered if he would be so keen when he saw me. Katie said I looked as if I'd been fifteen rounds with Muhammad Ali, but when I caught a glimpse of myself in the mirror I thought I would have looked better if I had. My right eye was swollen and becoming progressively more black, and there were several grazes arranged decoratively around my nose and left cheek. I tried to convince myself that they looked far worse than they actually were.

I put Katie on the train at Harrogate station and then headed off towards Leeds to pick up the motorway. Driving over the top of the Pennines, the rain lashed down on the windscreen and the wind tugged relentlessly at the steering wheel, as if trying to drag me into the bleak abyss either side of the road. It was a self-centred thought, but I would have hated Harry's car to have given up on me, especially in the middle of nowhere.

In the end I was quite surprised just how little time it did actually take to get to Stockport. I was there just before noon – but then it took me another hour to find Michael's flat.

'Bloody hell!' was all he could say as he opened the door to let me in. When he'd recovered from the initial shock, he ushered me through a small hall and into the living room. He fussed like a mother hen.

'Don't worry, Michael, it looks far worse than it actually is.' Surprisingly, it was quite easy to say.

'Let me get you a drink.'

'Coffee would be fine.'

'Nothing stronger? You look as if you need it.'

'Just coffee,' I insisted.

Michael disappeared out of the room and I heard a second door open, then the sound of running water. Inquisitive as ever, I stood up and popped my head out into the hall. Apart from the lounge door and one half-opened into the kitchen, there were three others visible.

'Where do these lead to?' I shouted above the noise of the water.

'Two bedrooms and a bathroom.'

I turned back into the lounge and waited for coffee to arrive. The room was adequately furnished, but nothing spectacular. The focal point was a rather grand piano at the far end, with a framed picture of Wellington Day perched on top. The whole thing looked a little out of place amongst the teak and dralon, but then I suppose it was typical of a bachelor pad. I moved to the window and looked out over a row of old semi-detacheds. The block of flats itself was new in comparison; I guessed it was probably nine or ten years old. Michael's flat was on the third floor with one more floor above it. I momentarily wondered how he had managed to get the piano up.

'Classical view, isn't it?' Michael came in carrying a tray of coffee and sandwiches.

'Come on then, tell me what happened.' He poured out the coffee and passed me a sandwich while I started to tell the tale. His expression throughout read something like 'you must be madder than a hatter', but when I got to the end where the girl gave me the name his expression changed dramatically. His eyes narrowed and his voice dropped to a concerned whisper.

'You're not going after Frankie Allen, are you?'

That took me by surprise. 'You mean you know who he is?' If Michael's voice was a whisper, mine in comparison shot up a couple of octaves.

''Course I do, don't you?'

'No, I've never heard of the man. Who is he?'

'It's not so much who he is, as what he is that concerns me.'

'Come on, Michael, what is he then?'

'To all intents and purposes he's a bookmaker . . .'

'How do you mean, "to all intents and purposes"?' I interrupted.

'Well, he owns a fair number of betting shops throughout the North, even some in Scotland, I think. But from what I hear, the best way of summing up his occupation would be "gangster".'

'Oh, come on, Michael, this isn't Chicago . . .'

'David.' This time it was his turn to interrupt and the urgency in his voice almost frightened me. 'I'm not joking. Frankie Allen is an extremely dangerous man.'

The afternoon was spent talking about all sorts of things, ranging from Frankie Allen to Michael's plans for Wellington Day. Michael was anxious to convince me not to get involved with the North of England's answer to Al Capone and, to add weight to his case, said I could get independent third-party advice from the club that evening. As for Wellington Day, he explained that the horse was now having a rest and would probably run next at Cheltenham on New Year's Day.

'Won't that be a difficult race?' I asked, already wondering if I should back it.

'Well, it will be hard because some of the top novices could well compete, but I might as well find out just how good he really is.'

'What does your trainer think?'

'Still thinks he's one of the best hurdlers he's ever trained, but I'm sure all trainers are optimistic by nature, if only to keep their owners happy.'

Michael wasn't due at the club until nine that evening and, since it didn't sound the sort of place for a meal, we popped out at six o'clock to pick up a Chinese takeaway.

A quarter of an hour later, as I tucked into my sweet and sour pork, I made the mistake of making a very slight reference to my past.

'Do you know, Michael, it's absolutely ages since I had a Chinese. I'd quite forgotten how much I enjoy it.'

'Where were you last time?' His question was asked in a very matter-of-fact way, and although I really couldn't remember the exact location I suspected it was probably somewhere in the Midlands. I didn't want to bring up my Wolverhampton connection, particularly since Michael had met Elaine, but now he'd got me talking about my past he was obviously going to start digging a bit deeper. I thought it was probably time for some sort of minor explanation.

'David,' there was a pause and then came the inevitable, 'do you mind if I ask you something?'

'No, go ahead.'

'What exactly are you doing working in that tiny little betting shop? I mean, you're obviously an intelligent sort of guy and you're definitely determined, otherwise we would never have met in the first place. I mean, why haven't you got a proper job?' He shifted uncomfortably in his seat, obviously finding the whole thing embarrassing, but on the other hand, if I had been in his position, I too would have been more than a little interested to discover the background to my relatively new-found friend.

'The reason I work in the bookies is simply because Harry Green-away was the first person to offer me a job after I lost my previous one, and probably if this business hadn't happened with Arthur's wife dying, I would more than likely be out looking for something a bit more suitable.'

'What happened to your last job?' Again the uncomfortable shift in the chair.

I'm sure he expected me to say I was made redundant or something like that, but I decided to be fairly truthful. 'I think you might call it dismissal for gross misconduct.'

My pianist friend looked shocked. 'What the hell did you do?' he croaked.

'Would you believe I knocked off the boss's wife?'

'The boss's wife?' he repeated, almost as a question.

'Well, actually, the Managing Director's wife.'

'Oh bloody hell, David.' There was a definite smile in his voice. 'I suppose if you're going to go out, you might as well go out with a bang!'

'I did, quite literally,' I answered, and suggested that we went out for a drink.

'We might as well start making our way into Manchester,' he said, still trying desperately hard to stop laughing.

Nothing much more was said as we walked down the stairs and into the open area which served as a car park for the flats. We got into Michael's car, and as we pulled out into the road he suddenly turned to me and said, 'Was she worth it?'

'Who?' I asked, slightly surprised.

'The Managing Director's wife?'

'Difficult to say, really. I must admit I did enjoy the relationship while it lasted, but then again I wasn't too keen on being unemployed. Still, I suppose if it hadn't happened I wouldn't have met Katie.'

'And what about Katie? How does she figure in all this?'

'She figures fairly prominently, in fact extremely prominently. To be honest, I don't know what I'd do without her now.'

'David, if you're that keen, why get involved with Frankie Allen and risk getting hurt?'

There he was, back to the 'don't go near the gangster' bit, but having gone this far I had no intention of being put off, especially since I felt at long last I could actually be getting somewhere.

'Michael,' I said, in a fairly resigned voice, 'from what I've told you, do you think Arthur's wife was killed, or am I just blowing the whole thing up out of all proportion?'

'Okay, so at first I did think you were getting carried away a bit, but now Frankie Allen's name has been added to the equation I'm not so sure. The man's certainly got his crooked finger in an enormous number of pies.' As if by afterthought he added, 'But I will tell you one thing . . .' He looked towards me as if asking permission to continue.

'What's that?'

'I don't think the guy you're looking for is called Davidson.'

'No, I tend to agree with you. Davidson, or whatever his name is, would have been crazy to use his real identity. So who do you think it could be? Frankie Allen?'

'Wouldn't surprise me a bit.'

By now we were driving into the centre of Manchester, and Michael negotiated the streets with an expertise which obviously stemmed from a local knowledge. We parked on a meter apparently quite close to the club. In fact Michael informed me we had driven past it to find the parking space. I certainly hadn't noticed it. As we approached the door, I had serious doubts as to whether there could be anyone inside; after all, who on earth would know it existed?

It was not how I expected a club to look. My idea of a Manchester night club would have been a big neon sign, wide glass doors and sparkling lights illuminating the bouncers as you walked in. (Can there be such a thing as an illuminated bouncer?)

In fact there was none of that – no sign, only big heavy doors with the smallest of windows and a pitch black corridor; even the glittering lights were missing. The latter resulted in me very nearly falling head over heels down the stairs, despite supposedly being used to negotiating dark corridors at the flat. Anyway, after descending the half-a-dozen stairs a little quicker than I had originally intended, I found myself at the outer edge of a very large room absolutely heaving with people and filled with smoke (the room that is, not me). Through the smog I could just make out a bar at the far end. Between it and us there seemed to be an obstacle course of tables, haphazardly scattered in land-mine fashion. In the corner to my right there was a small stage which acted as a dance floor, or should I say disco floor, judging by the sort of music booming through the speakers. The clientele was fairly well mixed, with the youngsters tending to congregate around the stage and the middle-aged conserving their energy at the tables.

The temperature in the room was quite warm, yet some of the customers were still wearing their coats. Frankly I didn't blame them – if I had a coat I don't think I would have risked handing it in at the cloakroom. In all, the place had a definite seedy air about it but, strangely enough, I didn't instantly take to it.

I turned to check that Michael was still behind me as I didn't fancy finding myself in such a place on my own. But sure enough there he was, a stupid grin on his face.

'What do you think of it?' he asked, obviously knowing what reply to expect.

'Well,' I answered, struggling for the right words, but then diplomacy had never been one of my stronger points, 'it's not like the club you played in London. What on earth brings all these people here?'

'The "in place", I guess. It's always like this, although I think the fact that you can drink all hours helps.'

'But where do you play?' I looked around for sight of the piano.

'Not in here.' He smiled and led me off to my left, through a door marked 'Cocktail Bar'. A vision of the cocktail bar at the Hilton flashed into my mind, but needless to say this Manchester version was nothing like the real thing. The room had that down-market feel, but it was certainly an improvement on the 'den' we had just vacated. Some attempt at least had been made with the décor and the lighting was a little more subdued, giving the place that intimate feel. The tables and chairs were the same standardised job lot, but rather than a dance floor there was a large white piano slightly raised on a platform, with half a dozen of the high stools placed around it, similar to those at the bar. I could imagine customers having one too many and falling off both stools and platform, but Michael assured me no one ever died whilst he was performing; he didn't allow it.

This room was not exactly full; in fact a quick glance suggested the waitresses outnumbered the customers by at least two to one. Michael looked quickly around and caught the eye of a small, balding man over by the bar talking to two of the waitresses. As soon as the man saw Michael, he walked over and grabbed my companion's hand.

'Michael, my boy, it's good to see you again.'

'Maurice, this is a good friend of mine, David Simms.'

'Any friend of Michael's is always welcome here.' He grabbed my hand with both of his and warmly pumped it up and down. 'Have you come to listen to Michael play? It always boosts the takings when he's here.' He turned and beckoned to one of the waitresses. 'Come on, let me get you both a drink.'

I had a whisky and Michael decided on Coke, saying it was likely to be a long evening. We chatted for about ten minutes or so, before Michael decided it was time to get changed and earn his money. He started to leave, and then took a step back towards us. 'Maurice, would you do me a favour?'

'Of course, Michael, anything.'

'Would you tell David a few home truths about Frankie Allen?'

Maurice's expression changed instantly; he was immediately on the defensive. 'Why do you want to know about him?' He obviously had a distinct dislike of the man, judging by his tone.

'It's all right, Maurice,' Michael said, coming to my defence, 'David's not the police or anything like that. He just thinks Frankie Allen could be involved with an incident in London which ended with the death of an old lady. David's got this crazy notion of tackling Allen about it and he won't listen to reason.'

Maurice's instinct for self-preservation was replaced with a concern for my own well-being. He gave Michael one of those Jewish gestures of total resignation. 'Michael, you go and get changed. I will put David right about Mr Allen.'

The pianist disappeared off through a door by the bar and Maurice handed my now empty glass to a waitress who, as if by magic, quickly changed it to a full one. The club owner then took me back into the disco room and, without drawing attention to himself, focused my gaze in the direction of two big bruisers standing at the bar with pints in their hands.

'They are my bouncers, except I don't employ them. I hire them from a company owned by Frankie Allen.'

'I see,' I said, for something to say.

'No, I don't think you do,' Maurice said sharply. 'They cost me at least twenty times more than I would need to pay if I employed them direct. But if I don't use Mr Allen's agency, then they would come anyway and simply smash the place to bits.'

'Protection,' I said, the light now shining through.

'Yes, except of course it's perfectly legal. I hire bouncers from an agency. The fact that I pay a fortune for them is my problem.'

We walked back into the cocktail bar, and Maurice continued his story by telling me that many of the other clubs and pubs in the area were in the same position. However, the protection racket was only a small part of Allen's empire. Prostitution, illegal gaming, and it seemed that even Allen's betting shop chain had been built up by 'persuading' small outfits to sell, presumably on the cheap. Apparently it was not unheard of for small-time bookies to have regular fights break out in their shops for no apparent reason and then be hit for a number of large winning bets, all of which added to the incentive to sell.

Whilst Maurice was telling me all this, my mind drifted back to the day the brick had come through the window of Harry's shop. I remembered how upset he had been at the comparatively trivial incident, and thought how it wouldn't take much to persuade him to sell if he suddenly found himself losing heavily and having to suffer a hooligan element as well.

I decided Frankie Allen was a bastard and told Maurice so. But Maurice had saved the best for last.

'About eighteen months ago there was a very nasty situation brewing up here. One of the big operators from down South thought there were easy pickings to be had in the North, and decided he would corner the market. Anyway, one night five people were shot dead.'

I tried to put my eyes back in their sockets discreetly, but it was obvious that I was shocked.

'Four of them were Southerners and rumour has it that Frankie Allen shot two of them himself. Maybe he did, maybe he didn't, but whatever happened the boys in London decided to leave Mr Allen well alone, and I would strongly suggest you do the same.'

'Frankie Allen shot two people?' There was a perceptible degree of disbelief in my voice. 'Everyone seems to know about it and yet he's still walking around as free as a bird?'

'From a practical point of view, he is certainly capable of shooting anybody. He belongs to a gun club and I hear he's an extremely good shot, with both handgun and rifle. As for still being free, the man's not stupid; he takes great care to cover his tracks and I'm sure it would be almost impossible to pin anything on him. In a funny sort of way I suppose he did us a favour; at least we're not plagued with mobs from the South and, who knows, perhaps even the police are grateful for that.'

I sighed and shook my head. The whole thing seemed totally unreal; surely people like that didn't really exist? It also made me wonder how on earth I could possibly take on such a man.

As if to read my thoughts, Maurice said, 'David, whatever has happened, it's not worth jeopardising your own safety. As a friend of Michael's, I tell you Frankie Allen would not take kindly to anyone interfering in his affairs, so why not drop the whole thing, enjoy your life. Here, let me get you another drink.' He'd obviously sussed my weakness.

The barman filled my glass with a double whisky and Maurice went off to talk to some paying customers. It was then I realised that Michael was at the piano and playing. He looked quite the part in a dashing white suit with white bow tie. All he needed were the spats and the hat and he would easily have fitted into some thirties Chicago gin joint. I supposed I would have fitted in quite nicely too.

Although I smiled over at him, inside I felt depressed. Realism dictated I should abandon this stupid quest, but if I did I would have failed again. But then I still had Katie, and perhaps now I could get a proper job and use my money as deposit on a proper flat. Oh, what the hell! I didn't know what to do, so I bought yet another whisky and went over to the piano. By now the alcohol in my blood was beginning to reach my brain and the rest of the evening became a dull, vague memory.

It must have been quite late before Michael dumped me into his car and ferried me back to the flat. I woke up the following morning with a lousy headache.

'I think I'll just go and have a chat with him,' I said matter-of-factly over coffee, toast and aspirins. It was one of those out-of-the-blue sort of statements.

'Who?' Michael asked, with the same degree of vagueness.

'Frankie Allen.' I tried to maintain the come-day go-day air, fearing the effect my words would have on the musician. I failed miserably.

'What!' he exploded. I didn't answer, so he carried on. 'For goodness sake, David, you are joking, aren't you?'

'Er . . . no.'

'But you told me when we were coming back last night that you were giving up the whole crazy idea.'

'Ah well, that was last night, when I was smashed. But listen, Michael. Seriously, I'm not going to make any waves or cause any hassle, I just want to know for my own peace of mind what was going on with those letters, and I'll tell Allen that. There won't be any problems; I'd just like to have one more go before I finally give up.'

Michael shook his head with despairing resignation. 'You'll never get to see him anyway.'

'Ah now, that's the one thing I was always good at,' I said with confidence.

'What?'

'Getting appointments to see people; I used to do it for a living. Pass me the phone book.'

I looked up the telephone number of Frankie Allen's head office. It was mid-morning, as good a time as any, so I dialled the seven digits whilst Michael looked on in disbelief.

The switchboard answered promptly so I put on my best 'give me an appointment' voice. 'Oh, good morning. Could you put me through to Mr Allen's secretary, please.' A couple of clicks and there she was on the end of the line. 'Oh, good morning,' I said again, 'is that Mr Allen's secretary?'

'Yes it is, can I help you?'

'I hope so. I'd like to make an appointment to see Mr Allen, please.'

'Who's calling?'

'I don't think he'll know me.'

From a fairly friendly start she became far more businesslike. 'Can I ask what it's in connection with?' she enquired.

'I've got a couple of betting shops I'm interested in selling, and I understand Mr Allen may be in the market for new acquisitions.'

Michael looked appalled and I was glad the secretary couldn't see his face.

'I see. Well, actually, Mr . . ?' I didn't volunteer the name so she continued, 'it's actually our Company Accountant, Mr Crossfield, you should speak to in the first instance . . .'

'I'm sorry to be a nuisance,' I interrupted, 'but if I'm going to sell these shops I would like to deal with Mr Allen personally. I'm sure you understand this is an extremely confidential matter, particularly when my staff know nothing of my plans. I really would like to see Mr Allen about it . . .' I paused, '. . . that is, if he's interested, of course.'

'Just one moment, please.' There was a click and then silence for thirty seconds or so. Michael was by now pacing around the room. A further click and she was back on the line. 'Mr Allen will see you at four this afternoon. Could I have your name, please?'

I pretended I didn't hear the last bit and just said, 'Thank you very much. Four o'clock it is then. Goodbye.' I replaced the handset and turned to Michael. 'Dead easy, wasn't it?'

'Dead's probably the right word,' was his only reply.

About an hour later, I got a call from Katie. She was in the office on her own and had decided to give me a ring. She told me she was missing me and said I should hurry home soon. It occurred to me that had she phoned before I'd fixed to see Frankie Allen, then I would probably have rushed straight back to London and forgotten the whole thing. But having got the appointment I thought I might as well go through with it.

So, at exactly five minutes to four, I walked into the reception of the Allen Organisation. Michael's parting words were, 'I hope you know what you're doing.' I hoped so too.

I looked at the brass plaques on the wall detailing the various companies controlled by the illustrious Mr Allen, and idly wondered which was the 'protection' agency Maurice had referred to.

Once in reception I announced I had an appointment with Mr Allen, and was taken up in the lift to the first floor by a man looking as if he should have been on the books of the bouncer agency.

The lift doors opened and we walked down a corridor considerably more opulent than the reception area, and I was shown into a room off to the right. A woman in her late twenties sat at a typewriter. She looked up as I walked in.

'Are you here to see Mr Allen?'

'That's right.'

'You didn't give your name on the telephone,' she reprimanded.

'Oh, I'm sorry,' I said, trying to sound surprised, 'it's Simms, David Simms.'

'Take a seat, would you, Mr Simms.'

I was sucked down into one of those very squashy leather armchairs whilst the secretary knocked on the door behind her, opened it and then disappeared inside. It was like something out of the Secret Service, although I guessed she was consulting with Allen.

The room I found myself in was quite large for the average secretary's office, and had a number of oak filing cabinets running the length of one wall. It seemed artificially bright for daytime, until I realised there wasn't as much as one window in the place. I didn't get a chance to notice anything else of possible interest to the aspiring Private Eye, because the secretary reappeared and instructed me to follow.

She showed me into a much more palatial room, with windows enough for the two offices and covered with those expensive vertical blinds. The room was tastefully decorated, with comfortable looking leather furniture, a drinks cabinet and oil paintings of racehorses scattered around the walls. I almost needed a leg up to step onto the deep-pile carpet, and I made a mental note to throw out the old peg rug back at the flat.

The grand surroundings didn't particularly surprise me; I had expect-

ed Frankie Allen to have expensive taste, but what did surprise me
was Frankie Allen himself.

He was sitting behind a large mahogany desk and didn't bother to
get up. He gestured to one of the leather chairs and I read his instruction to mean 'take a seat'. I did as I was asked and then just stared at
him.

He looked slightly uncomfortable. 'Is there anything wrong?' he
asked.

'I'm sorry, it's awfully rude of me to stare, it's just that you're . . . well
. . . not what I expected.'

He smiled. 'And what did you expect?'

'Well . . . someone older, I suppose. I'm not sure, to be perfectly honest.'

That was basically the truth. I wasn't sure what I had expected. I had-
n't given much thought as to what Frankie Allen would look like or
what age he would be. Perhaps subconsciously I assumed him to be
fairly old, maybe in his mid-fifties, yet the man behind the desk was
almost certainly younger than I was – I guessed somewhere in the region
of twenty-seven or eight. He was immaculately dressed in a dark blue
suit with a crisp white shirt and silk striped tie. I caught a glimpse of
his shoes under the table and reckoned he could have sold them,
bought out Harry Greenaway and still have had some change. His hair
was jet black, well-groomed and parted to the right. He looked more
like a merchant banker than a gangster or bookmaker.

'Mr Simms, would you like a cup of coffee?'

He had manners too. This was definitely not the Frankie Allen I
had imagined. I answered in the affirmative, so he pressed a button on
the telephone and, without picking up the receiver, ordered coffee for
two.

Then he leaned back in his chair as if to give me his undivided attention. 'Now, I understand you're interested in selling your betting shops.'

I took a deep breath. Talk about 'in for a penny, in for a pound'; I
felt as if I was in for the ton. 'Well, actually I'd like to sell them to Mr
Davidson, Mr C. A. Davidson. You are Mr Davidson, aren't you?' I
said it more as a statement than a question but, I had to admit, he
looked totally confused.

He straightened up in his chair. 'I'm sorry, I don't understand.'

'I'm trying to find Mr C. A. Davidson,' I spoke slowly and deliberately, 'and I think C. A. Davidson and Frankie Allen are one and the
same.'

I noticed his hand move slightly under the desk and, within a couple of seconds, a door I hadn't previously noticed opened and another
very smartly dressed man walked in, only this one was the size of the
proverbial brick outhouse and looked all muscle. I assumed Allen had

pressed some sort of alarm button, but for the time being that was as far as it went. The bookmaker motioned to the man to stay where he was, and it was obviously more than the henchman's job to disobey an order.

As I looked from one to the other, I began to realise that the whole business wasn't such a good idea after all. I sincerely wished I had taken Michael's advice - given the whole thing up before finding myself in such a mess. Above my own heartbeat the only thing I could hear was the tick, tick, tocking of the wall clock, as if counting down the seconds for my hourglass to run out.

The silence could only have lasted for a very short time but, like a condemned man, it felt like hours. I almost jumped out of my seat when I heard the door behind me open, but was relieved to see it was only the secretary bringing in the coffee. Her entrance seemed to ease the tension a little, so I thought I might as well try and lighten it even further.

I looked across at the tall, silent character and then back to Frankie Allen. 'I don't suppose he's your Finance Director, is he?'

The big man didn't even bat an eyelid, but Allen actually laughed. And it wasn't the sarcastic laugh I might have expected; he genuinely seemed to think the remark funny and then, to my surprise, he got up and poured me a cup of coffee.

'No, Les may be a lot of things, but he's certainly not my Finance Director. In fact, I am my own Finance Director, as well as Managing Director and Marketing Director. Les, for want of a better expression, is my Personal Assistant in the more, how shall I put it, delicate matters of business. He helps me when I feel a situation isn't totally within my control,' he paused, 'and I feel that at this moment.'

I knew I was completely out of my depth and decided that honesty was probably the best policy. Problem was, how to put it? By this time my first and foremost objective was to get back safely onto the streets of Manchester, preferably without Frankie Allen taking out a contract on me, or whatever it is they do in the movies.

I reached into my pocket and took out a cigarette. If ever I needed one it was now. 'Do you mind if I smoke?' I asked out of courtesy and an instinct for survival.

'Yes, I do, as a matter of fact.' Allen glared at the offending packet in my hand. I stuffed it quickly back into my pocket before Les could stuff it anywhere else. 'It's taken me two years to give up smoking,' Allen continued, 'so now I don't allow anyone to smoke in my presence. You should give it up, it's not good for your health. Here, try one of these.' He opened a drawer in his desk and took out a packet of what looked like chewing gum, and threw one over to me. 'It's designed especially to stop you wanting a cigarette,' he explained. 'I found it was the only thing that worked for me. The only trouble is, this particular brand is difficult to get hold of for some reason.'

Under the circumstances I felt honoured that he had actually offered me a piece of gum. I slipped it out of the plain cellophane wrapper to reveal the usual foil paper, except in this case it was bright green, almost iridescent. I put the gum in my mouth and the paper in the bin and chewed to keep my jaw from wobbling.

'Good, isn't it?' Allen half said, half asked. I nodded my agreement, even though I was still desperate for a cigarette.

'Of course, you need to keep chewing the stuff for days on end for it to take complete effect.' He unwrapped a piece for himself, passed me the coffee and then sat back in his chair and just looked at me. Obviously he was expecting some sort of explanation. I could feel my hands shaking a little and wondered if I could get the coffee to my lips without spilling it.

Although my nervous tension was obvious, I felt it was possibly to my advantage. I certainly didn't want him thinking I was some cool, calculating sort of character trying to stitch him up, as they say.

'I think I should put my cards on the table,' I said in my best he-man voice. Frankie Allen said nothing; he just took a sip of coffee and waited. I noted that his hands were not shaking. 'First of all, I don't have any betting shops to sell, but I do work in one, and over the last two months or so Mr C. A. Davidson has sent a number of extremely good tips to an old man I work with.'

'Why should he do that?' Allen asked quickly.

'He covered the first one with a letter explaining that he was a professional gambler and that he wanted Arthur, that's the old man I work with, to put some bets on for him. The finale of all this was supposed to be one absolute certainty that was going to win everyone a fortune. And, sure enough, the last horse did win, albeit very luckily, but then the letters went missing from old Arthur's flat and at the same time his wife died.'

I went on to explain the circumstances surrounding Mrs Clifford's death, and then a little bit of my detective work trying to trace this Mr Davidson. I finished by telling Allen his name had popped up in connection with some of the horses.

All the time I was telling the story, I had been watching Allen intently, looking for some sign of guilt, but again I had to admit either he was hearing it for the very first time or he was an extremely good actor.

When I finished, Frankie Allen didn't look at all happy, but he did turn to Les and dismiss him. I took it to be a good sign.

Allen poured more coffee and then asked a surprising question. 'Should I know you? Have we met before?'

'I'm certain we haven't; I would have remembered. Why do you ask?'

'It's just something about you that's vaguely familiar. But it's of no consequence.' He dismissed it with a throw-away gesture of the hand, but I was absolutely sure I had never met Frankie Allen before.

'So, you thought I was this Davidson character, the one behind the letters and possibly behind the old woman's death. What ever made you come and confront me like this? What could you possibly hope to gain, because if it was true and I was responsible for her death, I can assure you, Mr Simms, it is highly unlikely that anyone would have seen you again.'

I must have visibly tensed, because he went on to say, 'Relax, I had nothing to do with it, which means for the time being you're safe.'

'The time being?' I questioned, tentatively.

'The time being, meaning if you continue your, how shall I put it, investigations, and my name comes out to others as having some connection with this affair, then I will be very, very unhappy.'

'I take your point.'

'I hope you do.'

I believed him when he said he had nothing to do with the letters. I didn't want to, but I did. What still puzzled me, however, was his connection with the horses. So I asked him.

'Why should my name be linked to your tips?' He repeated my question as though I should have known the answer.

'Yes, why should it?'

'I would have thought that was obvious. I run a chain of betting shops. If I can get a reasonable idea of what's going to win the odd race, then as a bookmaker that puts me in a very advantageous position, wouldn't you say? I get information from many contacts and the set-up I have assures me that the information is reasonably accurate. How many horses did you say you were sent?'

I told him: five.

'I can get five tips in a day. The fact that my name happened to crop up with a couple of your horses is not really surprising.'

I didn't think it was a particularly convincing answer, but it was the best I was going to get. Frankie Allen showed me to the door and said he hoped we would not meet again. From the tone of his voice, I hoped so too.

Les appeared in the secretary's office and escorted me to the front door. I thought it was rather nice of him.

Once outside, I was just taking time to breathe a sigh of relief when suddenly to my surprise a car pulled up at the kerb beside me.

'Are you okay?' a welcome voice shouted through the car window. I looked down to see Michael's smiling face. 'Get in,' he ordered. I didn't need telling twice. I opened the door and sank into the passenger seat.

'You look as white as a ghost,' he said. 'Here, have one of these; you left them in the car last night and you look as if you could do with one.'

He held out a packet of cigarettes and instinctively I reached out to take one. It was almost between my lips when the little guardian angel in my subconscience dug in her heels. 'Well, how strange.'

'What is?'

'I don't want one.'

'I think you need one.'

'I probably do, but I really don't want one. That's amazing.'

'What on earth are you talking about?' he said, the exasperation beginning to show.

'Well, Frankie Allen has given up smoking and he wouldn't let me smoke either, but he gave me a piece of gum, reckoned it stops you wanting to smoke. I thought it was a load of nonsense at the time, but now I really don't want a cigarette.'

'Frankie Allen gave you a piece of gum?' he said slowly, as though I had finally flipped. 'This was presumably before he found out you hadn't any betting shops?'

'Funnily enough it was.'

I told Michael everything that had happened and finished off by saying that, in a strange sort of way, I quite liked the guy.

'Bloody hell, David!' Michael exclaimed, 'you can't like him, he's a killer! And anyway, I don't think he was being altogether truthful about getting the information on the horses. I found out something very interesting about Mr Allen this afternoon. He told you the information he gets on the horses he used in his betting shops.'

'That's what he said.'

'Well, I've been told that, amongst our Mr Allen's various business ventures, he actually runs one of those tipping agencies, if that's the right way to describe it.'

'You mean the sort of thing you see advertised in the racing press, send off a tenner or whatever and he'll send you a winner or two – if you're lucky.'

'That's about it.'

I thought it was a rather strange area of business for a bookmaker to be involved in, but what interested me far more was the possibility that one of his clients could be named Davidson. I didn't mention my thoughts to Michael, but then something struck me. 'Michael, what are you doing here?'

'I've been parked across the road watching to make sure you got out okay.'

'You're a hero,' I said, and meant it.

'What are you going to do now; do you want to come back with me?'

'No, I think I'll get back to Katie. Can you drop me at the multi-storey car park by Maurice's club?'

''Course. By the way, you don't fancy a day at the races on Saturday, do you?'

'I'd love it. But I thought you said Wellington Day wasn't going to run again until New Year's Day?'

'He isn't; I just fancy a day at the races, that's all. I was thinking about Nottingham – you could come up for the weekend; bring Katie too, if you like.'

I got out at the entrance to the multi-storey and waved goodbye as he drove off towards Stockport. As soon as his car was out of sight, I turned around and started to walk back towards the centre of the city.

It was just before six when I popped into the hardware shop. The woman behind the counter was just about to close for the night, but let me buy a small torch. Burglars need torches. I wondered if I needed anything else – I considered a sturdy screwdriver for prising open drawers or whatever else might need prising open, but I decided against it.

Back on the street, I made my way to the office block I had vacated earlier that afternoon. If Michael hadn't mentioned the tipster agency, I would very definitely have been on my way back to London by that time, but the hope that somewhere in Frankie Allen's building would be a record of all the people who had received tips was too good an opportunity to miss.

The trick was going to be breaking in and then rummaging through the various files without anybody realising it had ever happened. After all, it was a reasonable assumption that if Frankie Allen discovered he'd been burgled, he would put his Finance Director's hat on, add two and two together, and come up with Mr D. Simms. The last thing I wanted was Allen looking for me.

It was about ten past six when I arrived at the corner of the block which housed the Allen Organisation. My nerves were starting to get the better of me and I decided this was definitely going to be my last ditch attempt to find the elusive Mr Davidson.

I walked down the side of the building looking for an open window. A bit naïve, really. They were all firmly closed, but the front door wasn't; it was wide open. I walked past it, as any ordinary passer-by might do, and took a quick glance inside. A girl I recognised as the receptionist was just flicking off some light switches. I stopped at the side of the door with the pretence of lighting a cigarette and heard the receptionist shout, 'Gina, I'll get your coat; hurry up, will you?' With that, she walked down the corridor and disappeared into another room. Almost without thinking I slipped through the door and hid behind the reception desk. The girl walked back down the corridor and was joined by another, who I presumed to be Gina. They walked straight past my hiding place and out into the street, closing the door firmly behind them. A click signified it was locked.

This is too easy, I thought. Getting in had proved no problem at all; I hoped getting out would be the same. However, there was no point worrying about it at the moment. As I was inside, I decided to make the most of it. I maintained my position behind the reception desk for about five minutes, firstly to make sure I couldn't hear anyone else moving about, and secondly to let my eyes adjust to the dark. As soon as I felt safe, or at least as safe as I was ever going to feel, I made my way slowly up the stairs. It was pitch black and I was thankful I'd had the foresight to buy the torch. I was careful not to let the beam get out of control, so I went down the corridor like an usherette leading cinemagoers to their seats. My heart was beating like crazy, and I felt certain that if there was anybody within twenty yards or so they would hear it. I was not cut out to be a burglar.

I passed three doors, carefully listened at each and looked underneath, making sure there were no lights on. Everywhere was the same, quiet and dark.

I reached the door which I remembered to be the secretary's office, and stood with my ear pressed up against it for at least two minutes. Just because she had gone home didn't mean to say Mr Allen's office would be empty. But there was no sound of life, so I opened the door very slowly, willing it not to creak. I closed it behind me with an equal degree of care and stood in the blackness – of course, there were no windows. I wanted to get over to Allen's door so I could go through the listening ritual again, but I wasn't sure if I dared use the torch. Then again, I figured it was better than taking the risk of knocking something over.

The beam looked particularly bright and I made a vain attempt to shield it as I moved swiftly and quietly over to the door behind the secretary's desk. Another two minutes of intensive listening and peering under the door convinced me that Allen's office was also empty.

I switched my torch back on and went over to the filing cabinets. Gently I tried the top left-hand drawer, expecting it not to budge, but I was wrong; it opened with ease. I trained the beam onto the contents and decided it would be far simpler if I put the light on; after all, there were no windows.

I hoped against hope that what I was looking for would be in these particular cabinets, because I dreaded the thought of having to go through the same routine in every office. So I started on the contents of the first drawer, but no luck – it looked like staff files. The second was no better, with something equally mundane; but it was in the third that I hit the jackpot.

The drawer was full of files and a quick glance at the first showed details of a Mr Abel who lived in Crawley, Sussex. It showed how much he had paid, how often, and what tips he had been sent. It even showed how the horse got on.

I carefully replaced the file and moved straight on to the Ds; after all, this was obviously my lucky day.

I was so engrossed in looking for a file marked 'Davidson' that I didn't hear him come in. But then again, I shouldn't have expected to, and even if I had there would have been absolutely nothing I could have done about it. After all, Les was a professional.

The first thing I knew of his arrival was when this vice-like grip closed around my throat, effectively cutting off my air supply. I was virtually lifted off my feet and an enormous thump hit me in the kidneys. These two measures effectively took away any resistance I might have had, but his arm remained tightly around my throat whilst his free hand felt inside my jacket, presumably looking for a gun – what a laugh! The best he managed was my felt-tip marker pen!

It only lasted for about a second or two, and having discovered I wasn't armed with anything other than indelible ink, he flung me ten feet across the room. I hit the wall, back first, and with a considerable amount of force. I sank to the floor, but even though the room had started to spin I could see Les moving swiftly towards me.

With almost no effort at all he picked me up by the hair. I let out a cry of pain and saw his fist go back.

'Enough!' The shout seemed to echo around the room. Les simply let go of my hair and I returned to the floor in a heap. 'Put him in the chair,' the voice commanded, and Les picked me up and placed me in the same leather chair I had sat in earlier that afternoon. 'Check his pockets,' the voice commanded again. My head began to clear and my eyes focused again. The man who had spoken was Frankie Allen.

Les's fingers ran through my pockets like a hooker's through a client's, lifting everything they touched. He threw the contents down onto the secretary's desk.

Allen picked up my wallet and fished out my cheque guarantee card. 'At least you appear to be who you say you are,' he said.

Further delving confirmed that I lived in a flat in London and, as luck would have it, I even had a scrawled message on a piece of 'Harry Greenaway Turf Accountant' notepaper. All of these things seemed to reassure him that what I had told him about myself earlier was in fact the truth. He stuffed the various bits back in my wallet and returned it to my inside pocket.

'You're a very lucky man, Simms. Do you know that?'

I didn't feel too lucky at that moment in time and I told him so.

'In that case, I'll tell you why you're lucky, shall I?'

I nodded; it was all I could manage.

'You are lucky because at this present moment in time I can't really afford for anything to happen to you. If what you say is true, and I think it probably is . . .' He looked across at the files taken from the drawer. 'I see you were in the Ds. Looking for Davidson, I suppose?'

I nodded again.

'This afternoon you told me you'd been to the police about this woman's death. If anything was now to happen to you, there's a good chance the police . . . yes, even the police,' the sarcasm was now creeping in, ' might make the connection. After all, if you managed to connect this business to me, then it wouldn't take much for the police to do the same. Believe me, Simms, this is the last thing I want.'

'It would be ironic if you got done for something you didn't do, when you consider what you've probably got away with over the years.' I said it spontaneously, and then wished I hadn't.

But he laughed. 'So you believe I had nothing to do with this business then?'

'Oh yes, but I think you might hold the key.'

Allen turned to his Personal Assistant in the delicate matters, of which I was now one. 'Les, get us a drink, would you?'

Les immediately went through into Allen's office and came back with a bottle of Scotch and two glasses. I wasn't sure what I needed more, whisky or a cigarette, but of course I couldn't have a cigarette, so the whisky had to do. Allen poured me a generous measure, considering my predicament, and I knocked it back in one gulp.

The bookmaker sipped his drink and then took out his magic packet of chewing gum. If he hadn't offered me a piece, I would have probably asked for one, as the whisky only served to heighten my desire to smoke.

'First of all,' Allen said, 'how the hell did you get in here? I don't think you're anything more than an amateur part-time detective and that's being generous, yet you got in without triggering the alarms.'

'I walked in through the front door,' I said honestly.

'You what!' he exploded.

I explained exactly how I had obtained entry, and Mr Allen didn't look at all happy and told Les so. He also told Les to make damn sure it couldn't happen again.

'If I didn't set off any alarms, how did you know I was here?' I asked, almost out of idle curiosity.

'We were on our way out and saw the light shining under the door.'

What a moron, I thought. I take all the elaborate precautions of looking for a light shining under the door, and announce myself in exactly the same fashion!

'You really are a persistent individual,' Allen said, 'and I must admit

I don't know what to do with you.'

'You could always let me finish looking through those files.' I said it almost tongue in cheek. 'At least that way I'll either find what I'm looking for or I'll find nothing at all. In either case, you can then forget me for good, I promise.'

'Yes, all right,' he said calmly.

'Oh!' was the best I could manage.

'Don't sound so surprised. I've nothing to hide and, as I said, at this moment I can't risk anything happening to you. But, Simms, this is your last chance; don't push me any more.'

I knew he meant it this time and I assured him I understood. We moved over to the filing cabinets.

'First of all, let me tell you I have no customers by the name of Davidson.'

'Oh?' I said again, thinking that surely he couldn't know every one of his clients by name.

'I looked this afternoon, after you'd gone, purely out of interest.'

'Mr Allen, can I ask you something?'

'You can always ask.'

'Well, I'm confused about this tips service you run. Surely it's in direct conflict with your betting shops?'

'Well, of course, the two businesses are not compatible. I'd be bloody stupid, wouldn't I, sending out winners to punters who were going to back them in my shops?'

'Well, how can you stop them?'

'If you look through the files you'll notice there are two sections, both running from A to Z. The smaller file starts here,' he tapped the last two drawers, 'and in this section are the people I would prefer not to back winners, that is, people who live in the areas where I have my shops. If you notice, the addresses are all in the North.' He passed me a handful of files to examine. 'If you check the main section, the one you're standing by now, you'll notice that every single address is in the South.'

'I see,' I said slowly, 'so you send the good information down South and the people in the North get a load of rubbish.'

'That's about it.'

'There must be a hell of a lot of administration attached to it. Is it really worthwhile?'

'I'll say it is. It makes me a fortune. Northern clients send in money to pay for tips, I send them losers and a good percentage of them back the losers in my shops. Of course, they tend not to buy any more tips from me, although, would you believe, some do.'

I believed.

'On the other hand,' he continued, 'people in the South send in money, I send them a good percentage of winners, they back them with my competitors and then send more money for tips. In the majority of cases I can't lose, whatever wins. It's an extremely lucrative business, but of course I don't trade as Frankie Allen Bookmaker and, to be fair, I do only advertise the service in the Southern papers.' He smiled, obviously enjoying himself, but I just shook my head disbelievingly. What sort of character was this?

Allen returned to the drawer. 'On the assumption that none of my customers' names are going to mean anything to you, let's study it from a different angle.'

I looked at him, puzzled.

'Cross-referenced with the customers I keep a record of all the horses I get information on. Not all the clients get sent the same horses, so perhaps we can establish a pattern. You tell me the horses tipped and, if I have a file on them, I can tell you who I sent the information to.'

This was all too good to be true. 'Right,' I said, totally bemused by it all, 'the first one was Guide.'

'It doesn't mean much to me, but let's have a look.' He rummaged through a drawer and came up with a file. 'Ah, here we are: Guide. Won at six to one on the eighteenth of October.'

'That's right, my birthday,' I said, reflecting back to the day it had all begun. He handed me the file and directed me to a neatly typed list of names which ran into four sheets. None of the names meant anything to me.

'Okay, what's the next one?' he said, hurrying me along. I was quite amazed that his patience had lasted so long.

'Wellington Day.'

'Oh, Wellington Day.' He spoke slowly. 'Now, I do remember that one.'

I looked at him curiously. 'Why should you remember Wellington Day particularly?'

'When we get one which looks a real certainty, the boys who run this little operation on my behalf make sure they tell me, just in case I might have another use for it.' There was a mischievous tone to his voice.

'And you had another use for Wellington Day?' I interrupted.

'Yes, I did as a matter of fact. I'd been trying to buy a small chain of betting shops for some time but the stubborn old man who owned them just wouldn't sell. At the time Wellington Day was due to run, I figured he was fairly near breaking point, so I just helped him along – quite legitimately,' he hastened to add. 'I sent a few of the lads into his shops with some fairly hefty bets. At the same time, Les went off to the races with some even more hefty bets. A little synchronising of watches and just after Les put a few grand on Wellington Day at the racecourse, the boys put their bets on it in the betting shops, making sure they took the price on offer. Before the old man had time to lay off the bets, the odds had fallen like a stone. I think my boys got about six to one and Wellington Day won at something like . . .' he picked up the file to check, '. . . yes, seven to four.' He smiled. 'You see, these small bookmakers can't afford to lose the odd couple of grand, they just don't make enough. It's a shame, isn't it?'

'Underneath that façade you really are a bastard, aren't you?'

'It's the only way to get on,' he answered.

I checked the list of names associated with Wellington Day's file and again drew a blank. I also drew a blank with the others, until I came to the last one, and things took a slightly different turn. Brass Lock, good old Brass Lock, my fortune maker.

'Brass Lock?' Allen flicked through the files. 'No, I haven't even got a file for that one.'

'That's funny. You had a file for all the others and yet Brass Lock was the final tip, the absolute certainty, the one that was going to win us all a fortune. Are you sure there isn't a file? Let me have a look.' I almost pushed him out of the way, but he didn't seem to mind. If anything I got the impression he was beginning to find me strangely amusing. I searched through the drawer and, sure enough, there was nothing there for the horse.

'Hang on a minute,' Allen said, 'didn't Brass Lock win that race at Ascot when Towerstack and that other one fell at the last?'

'That was the race,' I confirmed.

'And you say you were sent Brass Lock to win?'

I confirmed again.

He rustled through a few more files and produced one headed Towerstack. He handed me the papers. 'Well, this is the horse which should have won that race, in fact it was probably a better bet than even Wellington Day. And what's more, I'll give you something for nothing: my informants tell me that Towerstack is possibly the best three-mile chaser that has ever lived. And believe me, they should know.'

I looked at him in surprise.

'Forget Arkle, Mill House, Pendil; Towerstack is unbeatable.'

'Well, Brass Lock beat him.'

'Admittedly. But it was a fluke, wasn't it?'

I agreed it was.

I flicked through the names of all the people who had been sent Towerstack as a tip, but not one meant anything to me. Then again, I didn't really expect them to. After all, Arthur had been sent Brass Lock as the winner.

'Are you satisfied now?' Allen asked, as I handed the file back to him.

'I think so.' The resignation showed in my voice. 'You can rest assured that I am, from this moment on, giving up the whole stupid business.'

'Good,' he said. 'In that case, why don't you come and work for me?'

At the time he spoke I was walking towards the door with the hopeful intention of leaving. But his question stopped me dead in my tracks. 'What did you say?' I thought I couldn't possibly have heard him correctly.

'I said, why don't you come and work for me? You seem like an intelligent guy, you don't mind taking the odd risk or two, you know a bit about racing and you know more than a bit about my set-up. You don't have a proper job, so it would make sense all round.' He paused. 'I could also keep an eye on you.'

The last sentence was said in a more light-hearted fashion, but I could tell he was serious about the rest of it. I was almost speechless. I was also very tempted. After all, I tended to think it would be quite exciting working for him. But on the other hand I could see the odd few drawbacks, like the chance of ending up behind bars, or behind the wooden lid of a coffin. And then there was Katie to consider, and I didn't think Michael would have been over happy, and Michael was by now a good friend.

'I'm sorry, Mr Allen,' I said, 'but I don't think it's for me.'

'Please yourself,' he said, matter of factly.

'But thanks anyway.'

'Where are you going now?'

'I'm going to drive back to London,' I said, not relishing the prospect of the long journey.

'In that case, Les will escort you to your car, just to make sure you get on your way.'

That confirmed my suspicions. Les was definitely sweet on me.

7

It was almost one o'clock when I parked outside my flat, and what's more, I had made the whole journey without wanting a cigarette. I decided I had to get some of Allen's magic gum. The only trouble was I couldn't remember what it was called.

I got out of the car and looked up at my window. I felt happier than I had for years, in fact I wasn't really certain I had ever been happier. Despite the driving I was extremely relaxed; it was like waking from a bad dream. Whoever this Davidson character was, it really didn't bother me any more. I had tried my best, done what I could, and it was pointless now trying to pursue the matter any further. At least I had found out why poor Michael hadn't made his fortune on Wellington Day the first time out – but not even that mattered any more, because Wellington Day was worth a great deal of money and Michael was happy.

I was still confused as to why Davidson thought Brass Lock was such a certainty when the rest of the racing world seemed to think Tower-stack was unbeatable. But why worry? I had won a lot of money by fluke, so I should sit back and enjoy it.

Only poor Arthur had come out of it badly, but probably his wife really had slipped, and as long as Arthur thought that he wouldn't be unnecessarily concerned. And at least he would be well looked after by Harry, Jim and Sylvia, and perhaps by me and Katie to a lesser degree, because I had now firmly decided to leave my lowly position as Assistant Boardman and get myself a more befitting job. Perhaps then I could persuade Katie to marry me.

I could just detect light shining through the curtains. I smiled to myself and thought how a week or so ago that observation would have worried me; I would have probably expected some violent criminal characters to be waiting for me to return. But now I knew it would just be Katie.

I felt my way carefully up the dark staircase and quietly inserted the key in the lock. Katie was lying in bed with an opened book on the floor. She had obviously fallen asleep with the light on. I crept over, feeling a little like Prince Charming– minus the tights – and kissed her softly on the lips. She awoke with a start, leapt up and hit my nose with her forehead; hardly the romantic encounter of the century! But I didn't care, I just wanted her to know how much she meant to me. I took her in my arms and held her for what seemed an eternity.

'David . . ?' she whispered, running her fingers through my hair as we lay on the bed.

I pulled away slightly and lifted her face up towards me. Her expression was so serious, so intense, that I felt sure she was about to say something profound, something which to me would be of immense importance.

'What is it?' I asked, willing her to say the right words.

'I do care . . .'

I felt a warm glow inside. It wasn't quite what I wanted to hear, but it was a start.

I told Katie that I had decided to abandon the part-time sleuthing. I also told her, in general terms, what I had found out, detailing the meeting with Frankie Allen and Les, but what I did not mention were the burglary exploits. I was careful to construct the story about Allen's shadier business dealings to make it sound as if all had been revealed during the afternoon meeting. I didn't think Katie would have been keen on my breaking into a gangster's lair, more from a concern for my safety than any moral issue. When I told her Allen had offered me a job, she very nearly had kittens. She sat bolt upright in bed and demanded to know what my reply had been – I quickly reassured her that I had declined. She commented on how my portrayal of Allen made him sound a likeable character, and in a strange sort of way that was how he had come across. But, nevertheless, I was astute enough to appreciate that he was a dangerous man, and behind that external veneer no doubt lurked a heart of stone.

'It certainly wouldn't surprise me if Maurice-the-club-owner's stories about the gang warfare were true,' I admitted.

'David, please promise me you will never get involved with people like that again.'

I promised – which all goes to show you shouldn't make promises you can't keep.

The following day I told Harry and Jim basically the same story. I also explained to Harry that I was going to look for a proper job. The general consensus of opinion seemed to be that I was doing the right thing, and not before time too.

Katie told me she would type the job applications, so during the morning I went out and bought a pile of newspapers with 'Situations Vacant' ads.

Walking back home that evening with the various papers stuffed into a carrier bag, my thoughts were of Katie. My concern was that she had never actually said she loved me, but she was obviously very, very fond of me. So was asking her to marry me a little bit premature?

Very confusing. I had never been in this situation before. I suppose there was also the fact that we hadn't really known each other for long. At least now that I had given up chasing the elusive Mr Davidson, I could spend a great deal more time with her and we could get to know one another better. Having weighed up the pros and cons, I decided to hold off popping the question for a couple of weeks.

I arrived at the flat about an hour before Katie, and had already scribbled out three or four job applications by the time she appeared. But that was the easy bit. When the application forms materialised I would be back to my original problem, with the inevitable question on each form asking why I had left my previous employment. But, of course, it was slightly different this time, because my last employer would be Harry Greenaway Turf Accountant, and Harry was more than happy to give me a glowing reference.

'Katie, darling,' I said almost flippantly as she walked in.

'Yes, David, darling,' was the equally flippant reply.

'I forgot to mention last night, I can't think why . . .' I added with a wicked grin, '. . . but how do you fancy going to the races?'

'I'd love to. I've never been before. When?'

'Saturday, at Nottingham, with Michael.'

'Oh David, I can't go on Saturday. With being away in Yorkshire last weekend, I really should go home on Friday; mother's not well.'

'In that case, how about me coming home with you instead? We can go racing another day.'

Katie took my hands and sat me down on the edge of the bed. 'David, when I say she's not well, I mean she is really ill. She has been for a long time.'

'What is it?' I asked, concerned.

'Bone calcification. It requires constant care. My dad's retired so he can look after her during the week, but I think it's only fair to give him a break at weekends.'

'But if I came with you, I could help.'

Tears formed in Katie's eyes. 'David, it's not just the physical illness but also the mental effect it's had on her. She is so wasted that having a stranger around would upset her terribly. Please try to understand.'

I reached up and wiped a tear from her cheek. 'Will she get better?'

Katie shook her head and moved across to the cassette player, her back towards me. I joined her and slipped my arms around her waist. 'It's okay,' I said softly, 'let me know when you think the time is right.'

'Perhaps a day around Christmas. I'll get her geared up for you coming then.'

For the next two nights Katie and I spent the time making love and writing letters for jobs. She borrowed a portable typewriter from the office and completed the applications beautifully.

On the Friday evening, Katie got dressed while I was still lying in bed freezing. On her way out she came over and kissed me. 'Tell you what, next weekend I promise I'll stay with you.'

I went down to the betting shop, taking my overnight bag with me, intending to catch a late afternoon train to Stockport, but at about eleven o'clock, just as I was pinning up the results sheets on the wall, Harry called from the office. 'David, Michael's on the phone.'

I went to take the call, which only lasted about a minute and resulted in my putting the receiver down probably a lot harder than I had intended. Harry looked up in surprise.

'Oh, bloody hell,' I said, and then qualified my minor outburst by explaining that my little trip to the races was off – Michael had been offered two nights' work at a club in Glasgow. He had offered to take me with him but, as I told Harry, the thought of a weekend in Glasgow didn't exactly inspire me.

'Does that mean you're working tomorrow?' he asked.

'Probably.'

'Well, I'll expect you if I see you, but don't worry about it if you find something better to do.'

'What a good boss you are,' I shouted back, and wondered if I would have found Frankie Allen quite so benevolent.

The walk back to my flat that evening was quite an eye-opener. Christmas! Until Katie had mentioned it I hadn't realised it was so close, and with my mind no longer on the Davidson investigation I began to notice a whole new world. There were pretty fairy lights, Santas in shop windows ...and Katie had even said I could go home with her at Christmas. Since childhood I had always loved the festive season – things were obviously looking up.

I woke up early on the Saturday morning and, having failed to get back to sleep, decided to get up and make myself a cup of coffee. The cream had gone off, so I dressed and went out to find the milkman. It was still quite dark outside and there was no sign of him, so I walked down the road towards the paper shop and it was there that I found him, chatting to the man behind the counter. Still, it meant I could kill two birds with one stone, so I bought a paper as well as the cream.

Walking back in the cold morning air reminded me of that unforgettable Saturday not so long ago, when I was trying to waste time before going to Ascot to watch Brass Lock's race. I suppose that thought sowed the seed and before long I had convinced myself that I really should go to the races regardless. The more I considered it, the more the idea appealed. It was about time I had a day to myself.

I didn't fancy going all the way to Nottingham, so I opened the paper at the racing page to check the alternatives. Nottingham, Cheltenham, Catterick and Lingfield. Lingfield was fairly close to London; that would do nicely. I made a quick about-turn and went back to the paper shop for the *Sporting Life*.

Once back in the flat, I made the coffee and started to study the form of the Lingfield runners but, as my eyes glanced down the page, they didn't get any further than the second race, a novice hurdle with twelve contenders, one of which was Ellerton Express. Elaine would almost certainly be there, so should I go or not? Damn it! I'd decided to go before I knew Ellerton Express was running and by this time I was really quite excited at the prospect of a day at the races. At least that's what I told myself.

I had another coffee and lit a cigarette. What the hell was the chewing gum called?

I phoned Harry out of courtesy to let him know not to expect me. I told him I was going to Lingfield and jokingly suggested he gave Frankie Allen a ring to get some tips. Harry was not amused.

I walked to the tube station and made my way to Victoria. From there I got the train to Lingfield.

I had never been to Lingfield before so, with plenty of time to spare, I took a stroll around, trying to decide if it was the sort of place to bring Katie. After only ten minutes of walking my mind was made up; this would undoubtedly be a good place for Katie's initiation into horseracing. I searched around for a quaint coffee shop, the sort Katie would like, and bought myself an early lunch. One of the waitresses tried to give me directions to the racecourse, but I eventually decided it would be simpler to get a cab.

Being race day, taxis were fairly easy to come by, and the one I caught took me right down the side of the grandstand and dropped me by one of the turnstiles. Very kind of him. Feeling lucky, I gave him an extra tip.

Lingfield Park is a pleasant country racecourse with the track itself not dissimilar to Epsom, having a downhill run very like the Derby course. However, I doubted if it would make too much difference to races over the jumps.

I bought a day badge for the members' enclosure, giving me access to all the public areas of the course and, since there was still half an hour to go before the start of the first race, I went into the main bar underneath the stand. I bought a whisky, lit a cigarette and made the final deliberations over my first investment. There were twenty-two runners and not one had any form to speak of. I might just as well have made my selection with a pin. However, I chose a horse without such an aid and then invested the princely sum of one pound, purely to give me an interest in the race.

The pound turned out to be a wise decision. The horse finished unplaced. I hadn't really taken a lot of notice of the race itself, since most of the time my binoculars had been trained on the crowd in the members' enclosure. Even so I hadn't spotted Elaine.

After the race I threw my betting slip in a bin and went back into the bar. Another whisky, another cigarette, and then I sauntered over to the parade ring. I took up position at the top of the tiered steps; that gave me the view I wanted, but also kept me well hidden amongst the crowd.

The horses were being led around by the various stable representatives, but my interest centred more on the owners and trainers just entering the ring.

Elaine was easy to pick out, her stunning features evident even from where I was standing. I focused my binoculars to get a closer look and also to check out the man she was with. I homed in on his dark, rugged face and recognised Duncan McKenzie, the trainer of Ellerton Express.

The jockeys filed in and then dispersed to their respective parties. Ellerton Express's jockey touched his cap as he greeted Elaine and McKenzie.

I wondered if they thought he would win; hopefully I would find out during the next few minutes. The jockeys went over to mount and the owners and trainers started to leave the parade ring. I stayed where I was and kept my eye on Elaine, just in case anyone else went to join her. Nobody did and, even better, McKenzie went off towards the stables, probably to check on his runner for the next race.

Elaine was now alone and heading towards the members' stand. Her progress was impeded by a small queue of people patiently climbing the stairs, and I was easily able to tuck myself in behind her. 'Well, should I back him?' I asked quietly.

She turned around, slightly startled, but then a smile broadened across her face. 'Hel . . . lo.' The word was spoken in two long drawn-out syllables and it had a definite welcome to it.

'Come on then, is he going to win or not?' I pressed.

'You should be interested in the sport, not the winning,' she teased.

'Oh, I am,' I answered, 'but I'm also interested in winning. So come on, is he going to?'

'He might do,' she said in the same tone, her eyes flashing with mischief.

'What sort of answer is that?'

'Well, Duncan McKenzie says he should certainly get in the first three, but he's a bit worried about Gladiator, the favourite.'

We had reached a reasonably uncrowded bit of the stand, and I focused my binoculars to check the odds on offer from the line of bookmakers below. Gladiator was two to one, Ellerton Express three to one, and then surprisingly a horse called Distribution was shown at six to one. I say surprisingly, because earlier that morning when I had studied the form, I hadn't given Distribution as much as a second look. It was his first run and according to the *Life* he wasn't likely to feature in the betting. Gladiator was well tipped, having won his last two races after finishing third first time out.

I pointed out Distribution's odds to Elaine, but she said she hadn't heard anything about the horse. Most of the runners were well on the way to the start, so I took the steps two at a time down into the Tattersalls. Ellerton Express had drifted in the market to four to one, so I placed my bet at that price and went back to Elaine.

'What have you backed?' she asked.

'What a daft question. Yours, of course.'

She smiled and asked how much I had put on.

'Twenty quid,' I said nonchalantly.

'Twenty pounds!' Her voice showed more than a little surprise. 'I can remember the days when we had heart failure if you put a fiver on.'

'Ah well, I'm on my way back up in the world now.'

The horses were circling at the start.

'Under starter's orders,' the commentator's voice boomed through the loudspeakers, and the race began.

We both stood with our binoculars fixed on the leading group of horses. They were all fairly well bunched.

'What instructions have you given the jockey?' I asked Elaine.

'I haven't told him to do anything. I tend to leave that to Duncan McKenzie. He suggested he should stay up in the first four, hit the front over the last hurdle and then win if he could.'

That sounded fine to me. And, sure enough, Ellerton Express disputed third place for about the first mile and a half of the two-mile race, but then coming up to the second last hurdle Gladiator took up the running and drew about four lengths clear. There was quite a long run to the last obstacle and Ellerton Express went after him with a vengeance. Approaching the last, Gladiator was only a length in front of Elaine's horse and the two were about four lengths clear of the rest. They jumped the last hurdle almost stride for stride but, a couple of yards later, Ellerton Express pulled into a two-length lead.

I thought I was about to become somewhat richer when suddenly, from out of the pack behind the leading two, Distribution appeared like a rocket with a homing device. With about fifty yards to run Ellerton Express was still in front, but the writing was on the wall – Distribution was gaining with every stride. In the end he had little difficulty in passing Elaine's horse and winning by a comfortable two lengths.

I lowered my binoculars and smiled.

Elaine look apologetic. 'It was a good race.'

'Yes, I suppose it was . . . but I've got an idea.'

'What's that?'

'Go and tell the jockey to object.'

'Object to what?' she laughed.

'Object to me losing!' I moaned, and then joined in her laughter.

Elaine went off to have a quick word with her jockey and trainer, and we met up again twenty minutes later in the members' bar.

'Cheers!' I said, lifting my whisky glass.

She raised her glass to mine. 'Just like old times.'

'I suppose it is really.'

'Oh, it is,' she confirmed, 'you screaming and shouting at the horses; standing in the bar after a race; even the horse you backed came second. Most of them did, didn't they?'

'I'm not so sure they all came second, but most of them didn't win,' I had to admit.

It could so easily have been eighteen months earlier. Both of us together at the races, relaxed in each other's company. And I was relaxed – the circumstances should have told me not to be, but three whiskies can easily anaesthetise the brain.

'It's a good job I was on my own,' she said.

'Well, I did check first.' I tapped by binoculars. 'Is George ever likely to come?'

'No, he's not the slightest bit interested, and anyway he's in New York at the moment.'

'What on earth's he doing in New York?'

'Trying to move into the big time, I think.'

'I thought he was already there.'

'There's a difference between being "big" in Wolverhampton and being "big" in New York,' she said knowingly.

'He's not thinking of going into newspapers in the States, is he?' I asked, surprised.

'Oh no, I think it's just a meeting, but then I take about as much interest in his business as he does in my racing. But let's not talk about him. I really am very glad you came today.'

And in a stupid sort of way I was pleased to see her too.

Four races later I still hadn't backed a winner, but at least I hadn't lost anywhere near another twenty pounds.

As we walked out of the course I began thinking about an evening on my own in the flat, and on the spur of the moment decided to ask Elaine if she fancied having dinner. And she did. Oh Katie, why did you have to go home?

We got into Elaine's Porsche and headed back towards London. It was easy to park just across the road from my flat, and from there it was only a short distance to a reputedly decent Italian restaurant. Elaine had suggested popping into the flat to freshen up first, but I didn't think it would be a good idea and steered her away from it.

As we entered the restaurant, a waiter showed us to a candle-lit table and Elaine immediately excused herself to 'powder her nose'. I ordered yet another whisky and tried to concentrate on the menu. She was back in a few minutes. I watched her glide across the room, waiters dashing to move chairs from her path. I smiled to myself; nothing had changed, especially Elaine's good looks. After her visit to the powder room, her long blonde hair was no longer tied back but flowed loose around her shoulders, and she had removed her coat to reveal a simple blue dress and a figure I remembered so well. I took a deep breath and resolved not to drink any more.

Elaine was followed by a bottle of champagne.

'I didn't order that,' I said, surprised.

'No, I did,' my beautiful companion said, ' just for old times' sake. But you'll probably have to drink most of it; I'm driving, remember?'

Throughout the meal the memories cascaded to the surface like the bubbles in my glass – good memories of happy times. On a couple of occasions our hands touched across the table; that brought me back to earth and, in an effort to break the spell, I tried talking about Katie. Unfortunately the alcohol made it difficult to concentrate on anything for more than thirty seconds at a time.

We strolled back through the freezing night air and paused beside the Porsche. 'I'd better go,' Elaine said, almost apologetically.

I nodded and opened the car door, grateful that I didn't have to find an excuse to stop her coming in. I wanted us to part the good friends we had always been, because I knew I would never see her again.

'Take care,' I said firmly, and then walked quickly across the road, careful not to look back.

The front door was unlocked as usual; the Yale catch had been missing for as long ago as I'd lived there. Pausing in the darkness of the hallway, I took a deep breath before slowly tackling the stairs. I had actually reached my door when I heard the footsteps behind me, and turned to see Elaine rushing after me as fast as her elegant shoes would allow. She had a package in her hand.

'David, I've caught you,' she gasped. 'I wasn't sure which flat you lived in . . . you might need these.' She held out my binoculars then leant against the wall to catch her breath.

I took them gratefully, opened my door and switched on the light. 'A quick coffee before you go?' I turned for the answer just as Elaine followed me in. There was a minor collision and a duet of surprise but our faces were left no more than a few inches apart. In that brief second the physical side of our past came flooding back as if it had never been away. Our lips met but before the kiss ended our hands were entangled in each other's clothes. There was no commitment, but there was also no stopping.

I was first to wake in the morning. I could see it was already light out-side. At first I thought it was Katie beside me, but then the memory returned like a ghost from the night.

I looked at my watch; it was almost ten. My mouth felt dreadful and my head was little better. I vaguely wondered how much alcohol I had consumed – obviously far too much. I slid quietly out of bed and put some clothes on.

As well as feeling ill I felt desperately guilty. The whole room was Katie. What the hell was I doing with another woman in our bed? How on earth could I have been so stupid?

Elaine woke up with the sound of water splashing into the kettle.

'David, this place is absolutely freezing,' she said sleepily, as she crept further under the bedclothes. 'How on earth do you live in it?'

'I suppose I'm used to it by now.'

But it really was cold; in fact there was ice on the inside of the win-dow. I handed her a cup of coffee and sat on the bed. 'Elaine,' I said, taking a deep breath, 'I'm not going to be able to see you again.'

She sighed, and then leaned forward to kiss me on the cheek. 'I understand . . . At least you seem to have something going for you, and I don't want to ruin it. After all, I've got what I started out to get, the money and the lifestyle. It's a bit unfortunate it happens to be accom-panied by George, but still, that was my decision.'

By a quarter to eleven we had eaten toast and drunk a lot more cof-fee, the latter mainly to keep warm. Like the good little housewife I was fast becoming, I even washed up the cups and plates and tidied the room, while Elaine got ready to leave.

And then it happened.

Elaine had just buttoned her coat when the door opened and Katie walked in. She was obviously about to say something, because her mouth had opened, but the sight of Elaine rendered her speechless. Still, I must say the sight of Katie had exactly the same effect on both Elaine and me.

My first thought was that at least the bed was made and Elaine had her coat on. It should be okay. I must have looked guilty, but then what exactly does a guilty man look like?

Elaine recovered first and, to be fair to her, she did very well given the impossible situation. 'Hello, you must be Katie,' she said. 'I was just passing and popped in to say hello to David. I was just going.' She moved towards the door and Katie stood aside to let her through.

'This is a nice surprise,' I said, trying to sound as natural as possi-ble.

'I bet it is.' Katie's voice was understandably harsh. 'I came back early because I felt guilty leaving you on your own. I see I needn't have worried.'

I tried to reassure her, desperately wishing I could undo the last twenty-four hours. 'Katie darling, she only dropped in as she was passing.'

Katie walked over to the window and looked down towards the street. 'Nice little sports car she's got there.'

I heard the engine explode into life and roar off up the road.

'You are a bastard, David, you really are.' She burst into tears and then shouted, 'I'm surprised she could start the bloody thing with so much ice covering it.'

'Oh Katie . . .' I moved towards her with my arms out, but she ran through the door, slamming it behind her.

By the time I reached the top of the stairs, she had gone. I hesitated, wondering whether to run after her, but decided it would only make matters worse. I went back into the flat and kicked the waste paper bin across the room, then flung myself down on the bed in desperation. What on earth was I going to do? How would I ever get her to forgive me when, in the harsh light of day, I couldn't forgive myself?

After much deliberation I decided to wait until about two o'clock and then go round to her flat. Hopefully by that time she would have calmed down a little.

By one o'clock I couldn't stand it any longer. I had tried the cassettes but they all reminded me of Katie. I couldn't concentrate to read and my splitting head didn't help, so I decided to go and see her.

The walk took about forty-five minutes. I'd hardly ever been to Katie's because we had always used my flat as a base, but fortunately she had given me a key in case of emergency. And this was definitely an emergency!

On the way I bought a big bunch of flowers – I didn't think it would exactly put matters right, but at least it was a gesture.

Katie's flat was similar to mine, except it was on the first floor. I let myself in through the front door and took the stairs three at a time. I opened the door to her room without knocking, but was amazed to find it empty. And when I say empty, I mean empty. The drawers and cupboards were open, and everything had gone. It all looked so desperately final.

I clung to the faint hope that she just might have packed everything to move in with me and we had crossed on the way. Bit of a stupid thought, really. Still, I ran all the way back to my flat, only to find it exactly as I had left it, with no sign of Katie.

Sitting on the edge of my bed, I tried to decide what to do. If she had actually gone in the complete sense of the word, then the only place she could go would be her mother's in Bristol, but of course I didn't have a clue where her mother lived. I hoped that maybe there would be some indication in Katie's flat, perhaps a letter or something.

In sheer desperation I ran all the way back again and searched from top to bottom, but nothing. Katie had left without a trace.

My mind was in turmoil but I did my best to get a hold of myself. What next? I wondered. I hadn't found Mr Davidson, but I'd had a damn good try, and at least I knew what Katie looked like. I also knew that she lived in the Bristol area. Armed with so much information, surely I would be able to find her?

The next fortnight was dreadful. It was one thing looking for Davidson through anger; it was quite another looking for Katie through despair.

The day after she left, I told Harry what had happened. He called me a prat, but nevertheless said I could use the phone, car or whatever I needed if it would help me to find her.

I spent three mornings ringing every single 'Brown' in the Bristol telephone directory. I simply asked the people who answered if I could speak to Katie, but not one gave any indication of knowing a Katie, let alone one living there. I tried Katie's landlord and also the temping agency she worked for, but had no joy from either. Over the weekend I borrowed Harry's car and drove down to Bristol. For two days I wandered around the city centre and drove through housing estate after housing estate. Although I knew what she looked like, the fact that I hadn't got a photograph of her didn't help.

Of course the weekend was a complete waste of time. It would have required more than an amazing stroke of good luck to have walked into her, more like Divine Intervention, and I could hardly see Him being on my side. Anyway, there was no guarantee she actually lived in Bristol – there seemed to be hundreds of surrounding villages; she could have been anywhere.

If I thought Davidson was an obsession, then I really couldn't have known the meaning of the word, because Katie, or at least the memory of Katie, simply took over every moment of my life. Each evening I couldn't face going back to the flat because it reminded me of her, so after I finished work I just spent the time wandering aimlessly around London. I didn't seem to think or do anything specific; I just walked and walked and only went back to the flat, usually very late at night, when I was absolutely exhausted. Even then I would rarely sleep, and when I did I just dreamed of Katie. Usually I dreamed of her coming back, but when I woke up and realised it was just a dream that made it all the worse.

I started to lose weight because I wasn't eating properly, and I was drinking far too much. Most days I couldn't see the point of going on, and yet I clung to the faint hope that perhaps at Christmas Katie might just reappear; after all, she had said I could go to meet her parents at Christmas.

There was no racing on Christmas Eve and I turned down the invitations from Jim, Harry and even Arthur to spend Christmas with them. I just stayed in the flat and worked my way through a bottle of whisky.

At four in the afternoon I was lying on my bed half smashed, when there was a knock at the door. My heart started to pound; I leapt up and virtually flung it open, but my face dropped as quickly as it had lit up. 'Hello, Michael,' I said dejectedly.

'Well, don't sound so pleased to see me,' he said, and then took a closer look. 'Bloody hell, David, you look awful!'

I must have looked like a tramp, but I didn't care. Michael came in and helped himself to a glass of whisky.

'What are you doing here anyway?' I asked, wishing it didn't sound so unfriendly.

'Harry phoned me,' he admitted. 'He told me what was happening, and as I hadn't got anything to do this Christmas I thought I might as well come and see you. We could go to Kempton Park on Boxing Day, see the King George Chase.'

'Yeah, why not? If it's one thing I have got, it's plenty of money to gamble with.' I looked across at the sideboard; there was about £300 in fivers sitting there. I had withdrawn it to continue my search for Katie, but it was obvious I wasn't going to find her and I was now quite sure she wouldn't be coming back.

Michael had booked into a hotel not too far away. He found us somewhere to have Christmas lunch and tried to sober me up a little, but I wasn't very good company.

On Boxing Day we went to Kempton. The King George Chase in terms of prestige is second only to the Cheltenham Gold Cup, and many of the country's top chasers were taking part. Michael had spent most of the morning studying the form for all six races, but I hadn't even bothered to look at the names of the runners.

For the first two races I didn't even have a bet; I couldn't see the point. I had very little interest in anything, but I did perk up slightly for the King George, particularly when Michael, with two dismal losers already under his belt, thrust the racecard before my eyes and insisted that I made some attempt to find him a winner.

I gave him a feeble half smile. 'Well, if Frankie Allen's right, then Towerstack must be a certainty,' I said, handing the card back to him.

'Oh, that's right. What was it Allen said to you?'

'He thought Towerstack was going to be the best three-mile chaser the world had ever seen, and if that's the case he should walk this.'

Michael checked the odds on offer with the numerous bookmakers.

'Two to one favourite Towerstack,' he said.

'I might as well have a bet then.' I turned and walked down towards the bookmakers, with Michael following on behind. He watched in horror as I put on £250 at two to one.

'What the hell are you playing at?' he asked, obviously furious.

'Well, I've got nothing else to do with it, have I? And if it hadn't been for Towerstack falling at the last fence at Ascot, I wouldn't have the money anyway. So what the hell.' I shrugged my shoulders and went back up into the stands. I really didn't care whether Towerstack won or lost; money was of little use to me now, except to buy whisky, and I already had a flat full of that.

Michael came up to join me, and out of mild curiosity I asked what he had backed.

'Towerstack,' he reluctantly replied, 'but only a tenner. I had to back it after you put a fortune on it. I could hardly have stood there and shouted for another horse, now could I?'

Towerstack hadn't run since that day at Ascot, but he had the same young apprentice jockey on his back. According to Michael's racing paper, the apprentice got on so well with the horse that he was also likely to ride him in the Gold Cup.

As the race started I could sense that Michael was nervous, but I knew his nerves were for me and my rather large investment. He needn't have worried, because Frankie Allen was right as usual. Towerstack was superb. I hadn't taken that much notice of him last time out, being far too intent on watching Brass Lock's disastrous performance, but there was no doubting it; he had the stamina of a bull and the acceleration of a Ferrari. He stayed at the back of the field for most of the race, biding his time, waiting for that right moment. Just before the second last he started to make up ground, and then cruised into an easy lead at the final fence and won in a canter by fifteen lengths.

Michael was delighted and, I must admit, it did cheer me up slightly. Three weeks ago, winning £500 would have had me ecstatic, but then again three weeks ago I would not have been stupid enough to put £250 on a horse.

After the racing had finished, Michael dropped me back at the flat, saying that he had to go back to Stockport because of engagements over the next few nights. He did offer to take me with him, but I declined. However, I did say I might go to Cheltenham with him for the New Year meeting to see Wellington Day run.

I went up to the flat and depression returned like a heavy shroud. I put the now much larger wad of money down on the sideboard, and again thought how little it meant without Katie.

The days between Boxing Day and New Year's Eve dragged intolerably. I spent my time mostly wandering and occasionally turned up at

Harry's shop. On New Year's Eve I didn't bother wandering. The last thing I wanted to see was people enjoying themselves. I stayed in the flat, and by seven in the evening I had virtually finished a bottle of whisky, so I got into bed and fell into a fitful sleep.

Michael came for me early on New Year's Day. He'd been playing in London the night before and looked tired. Even so, he didn't look half as bad as I did. The race Wellington Day was to run in was by far his most difficult, and would prove whether the horse was simply a good hurdler or, hopefully for Michael's sake, something very special.

As we drove down the M4, Michael told me he had turned down an extremely attractive offer to sell Wellington Day the previous week, and now the day of reckoning had come he wasn't sure he had made the right decision.

Michael was not a wealthy man by any means. The only reason he could afford to keep a racehorse in training was because of the prize money. As soon as he'd realised Wellington Day was a decent hurdler, he had been waiting for the right moment to sell him, hopefully at the peak of his value. As things stood the horse was reasonably hot property, being unbeaten in both of his two hurdle races, yet if Wellington didn't win today his value could plummet.

Losing was always a possibility, particularly since there were thirteen other horses in the race and no less than six were unbeaten over hurdles.

Michael had asked Tom Martin, his trainer, for an honest opinion of the horse and, although Martin had confirmed him to be the best hurdler he had ever trained, as trainers went, realistically Tom Martin was small time. Under the circumstances I could understand Michael's tension, and I began to feel a little guilty for being so absorbed in my own problems.

In an attempt to take an interest, and not having as much as glanced at the paper, I asked what the opposition was like.

'Well, a couple of weeks ago Tom Martin didn't think we had any dangers, but then a horse called Distribution had a good win in his only race to date, and apparently he's very well thought of.'

I resisted the temptation to say anything and pulled the *Sporting Life* off the back seat to look at the race in more detail. The reporter writing on the front page thought the contest was probably between four horses. In his summing up he came down on the side of Distribution, but suggested that Wellington Day would be a very close second. However, he did admit that it wouldn't surprise him at all if either Mile Post or Nova For Food won it. It was a very open race indeed.

By the time we reached Cheltenham racecourse I was getting as jittery as Michael, but at least it distracted me from my own troubles.

Michael had arranged to meet Tom Martin in the owners' and trainers' bar before the first race, and we were briefly joined by Carl Dixon, Wellington Day's jockey. He popped in just to enquire about the horse's well-being before dashing off to ride in the first.

We didn't even bother watching the first two races; instead we just sat in the bar, not drinking, just discussing tactics. In response to my questioning Tom Martin told me that, whilst Wellington Day had won his two races by running from the front and forcing the pace, he was convinced he would be even better if allowed to settle in the middle of the field and then come with a fast finish. 'After all,' he pointed out, 'Wellington Day is an extremely well-bred flat racer, basically designed for speed.'

I asked Martin if that was how he saw him running this time but he explained that, because the ground was on the sticky side with all the rain, it was probably better to have him up front throughout.

To an outsider the three of us sitting there must have looked a pretty morbid bunch, but the air was one of nervous tension rather than gloom, and certainly Michael was getting worse by the minute.

Tom Martin went off to help saddle Wellington Day, and Michael and I made our way to the parade ring. Some of the horses were already walking around and once again I was surprised at their size. Michael guided me to the gap in the rails and we stood there until all the runners were parading. The owners and trainers were beginning to gather inside the ring in their small, select groups.

'Come on,' Michael instructed,' come in with me.' He grabbed my arm and led me over to Tom Martin. Going into a parade ring was something I had always wanted to do. It was like being a part of the sport itself, like gaining entry to a very exclusive club. We stood virtually in the centre and, as I gazed out at the faces looking in, I thought that one day I would get a racehorse and become part of this fashionable world in my own right. Suddenly I realised I was almost looking forward to my future. Definitely a good sign.

Tom Martin told us that Wellington Day was three to one joint favourite with Distribution, Nova For Food was nine to two, but he wasn't sure about the others.

'Are you going to back him?' Michael asked, turning towards me.

'No, but not because I don't fancy him; I think I've already got too much on him emotionally on your behalf.'

'Thanks, pal,' Michael said with genuine affection, and patted me on the back.

The jockeys filed in and Carl Dixon, wearing Michael's red and gold quartered colours, quickly picked us out and walked over. Tom gave him his riding instructions and when the bell rang they both went over to Wellington Day, and the trainer gave the jockey a leg up into the saddle.

Carl Dixon was one of the country's leading jump jockeys. He was lying third in the Jockeys' League Table, but he was only half a dozen winners behind the leader. Michael was very pleased to have his services for Wellington Day, but on the other hand I got the distinct impression that Carl Dixon was equally pleased to have the opportunity to ride the horse.

Michael and I left the ring and pushed our way through the crowds up into the members' stand. By the time the horses reached the start it was packed solid and, despite the tiered arrangement of the steps, I was having to stand on my toes to get a view of the racecourse.

'They're under starter's orders . . .' the voice echoed through the loudspeaker system, *'. . . and they're off.'*

'Well, here goes,' Michael said, the stress by this time almost tangible.

There were eight flights of hurdles to be jumped and two miles to be covered. Wellington Day was quite prominent at the start, but after the group had travelled a hundred yards or so a horse called Golden Horizon sprinted off into a ten-length lead.

By the time they jumped the second hurdle and were running downhill away from the stands, he had increased his lead to about twenty lengths. The racecourse commentator took up the story:

'Out into the country, making their way to the third, it's Golden Horizon now twenty lengths clear of Wellington Day. This one heads the rest of the pack grouped closely behind.'

Michael put down his binoculars and was busy flicking through the pages of the *Sporting Life,* no doubt looking for the form page to get some idea of Golden Horizon's chances. It was always worrying when a horse careered off so far in front. Usually you could expect them to run out of steam well before the end and just fade away, but there was always the chance that one wouldn't.

'Looking for Golden Horizon?' I asked.

'Yeah, this is his third race. He was unplaced first time out and then he won a very low-grade race at Fontwell.'

'Nothing to write home about. Don't worry, he'll soon come back to the field.' I tried to sound reassuring and we both reverted to our binoculars.

For the next four hurdles the race maintained very much the same pattern, with Golden Horizon still well out in front and the rest of the horses, led by Wellington Day, in a bunch about fifteen to twenty lengths behind. But as they started to climb the hill on the far side of the course, it became obvious that the main group was starting to peg back the runaway leader. Halfway down the hill was the second last hurdle, then a long run to the final bend, followed by the last hurdle and a tough uphill trek to the finish. At this point I felt confident that things were going well for Wellington Day. They were approaching the second last and he was now only five lengths behind Golden Horizon. But having said that, he was only a length in front of another seven or eight horses who were bunched up behind him.

Suddenly a cry of anguish from Michael, and a few thousand other people who had obviously backed Wellington Day, shattered my optimism. Golden Horizon cleared the second last hurdle but somehow Wellington Day seemed to get his legs muddled and made a dreadful hash of the jump. He didn't fall, but he was very close to it and Carl Dixon did extremely well to stay in the saddle. Nevertheless, he lost a number of precious lengths and was instantly swallowed up by the horses following on behind.

I looked at Michael. He had lowered his binoculars as though it was all over. I wanted to say something, but I just couldn't find the right words.

With only one hurdle left to jump, the race was on in earnest. The leaders were vying for position and, although it was difficult to pick out Wellington Day, I estimated that he had dropped back to about seventh place and certainly a fair way off Golden Horizon, who obviously had no intention of relinquishing his position.

The horses swept round the final bend and straightened up for the last hurdle. Excited punters were shouting at the tops of their voices and waving their hands, papers and anything else they happened to be holding. I was finding it difficult to see, so I tuned my ears to the race commentator:

'*Approaching the last, and it's still Golden Horizon who's made it all three lengths clear of Nova For Food who's moved into second place, relegating Lightening back to third. Distribution now finishing well on the far side ...*' With Distribution entering the showdown, the crowd began to get even more excited. '*Over the last, Golden Horizon by two lengths from Nova For Food and Distribution who's still gaining. Wellington Day finishing well ...*'

It was almost as though Michael and I both received an electric shock at exactly the same time. We gasped and craned our necks forward in time to see the red and gold clad Carl Dixon absolutely flying up the Cheltenham hill.

'*Fifty yards to run and now very little between Golden Horizon, Distribution and Nova For Food, with Wellington Day still finishing fast. Up towards the line, it's Distribution, Golden Horizon, Nova For Food and Wellington Day all in line. They've gone past together. Photograph! Photograph!*'

I turned to see Michael, who looked as if he'd aged ten years in the last minute.

'I'll have to bloody well sell him; I don't think I could stand this again,' he said, with a pained look on his face.

'What do you think?' I asked, meaning the result.

'It's difficult to tell from here.'

'Wellington was finishing fastest of all and ten yards past the line there was no doubt that he was in front,' I said hopefully.

'Yes, but it's on the line that actually counts.' Michael stated the obvious.

We tried to push our way through the dense crowd in the stand to get to ground level and the unsaddling enclosure. It was very slow progress.

The results of photo finishes are usually announced quite quickly, but this one seemed to take an age. As if to read my thoughts Michael said, 'It must be very, very close.' A few minutes later we arrived in the relative open space at the back of the stands and started to run to the unsaddling enclosure.

'Here is the result of the photograph ...' the loudspeaker announced. We both stopped abruptly in our tracks. *'A dead heat for first place between number six Golden Horizon and number nine Wellington Day ...'*

We didn't hear the rest; Michael just flung his arms around me and shouted, 'YESSSS!' at the top of his voice.

'Put me down,' I joked, 'people will start to talk!'

'They can talk as much as they like. I don't give a damn.'

We dashed to the unsaddling enclosure and shook hands with Tom Martin. Carl Dixon came over en route to weigh in.

'I'm sorry about the second last,' the jockey said. 'If it hadn't been for that we would have won by a dozen lengths, but after the horse hit the hurdle it shook him a bit and I had to get him settled again before we could come with a run at the end.'

He started to leave, and then said to Michael, 'Mr Myers, you've got something very special in that horse.'

Michael turned to me. 'Perhaps I won't sell him after all.'

All the way to the bar Michael had a huge grin on his face, and who could blame him?

In the members' bar, Michael bought a couple of bottles of champagne. Tom said he would probably give the horse one more run, an easy one as he put it, before having a tilt in one of the major races at the Cheltenham Festival in March.

Later that afternoon Michael dropped me at the railway station and I caught a train back to London. Throughout the journey I reflected on what a fascinating day it had been. It was the first time I had ever been to the races and not had a bet, and yet it was the most exciting day's racing I had ever spent. I excluded the Brass Lock episode since that fell into the category of heart failure rather than excitement. My only regret was that I couldn't share this day with Katie. Oh Katie, where are you?

I had drunk about half a bottle of champagne on the course, but even though there was a bar on the train, I decided I didn't want another drink, and that could only be good.

I lit a cigarette. That's another thing which must go, I thought to myself. I really must make a concentrated effort to find Frankie Allen's magic gum.

I still missed Katie desperately, but I was now becoming resigned to the fact that she had probably gone for good. The feeling of depression which had trailed me for the past three weeks now seemed to be subsiding a little – I thought the worst was at last over. Wrong again.

8

I arrived back at the flat early that evening. There was three-quarters of a bottle of whisky sitting on the sideboard, so I put it out of sight just in case I was tempted.

I sat on the bed and looked across the room at the pile of unopened envelopes. I presumed they were all replies or application forms for jobs which, with Katie's help, I had written off for.

I went over and picked them up, counting the envelopes as I did so. Eighteen; not bad. If my memory served me right I had posted off forty-four applications, so eighteen replies to date seemed quite a good percentage. They had been falling quite regularly through the letter-box. I had never received so much mail in my life.

I started to open them one by one and browsed through the contents. They were all application forms and, even though the format was different in each case, the information they required was basically standard. I decided to start completing some of them although I guessed I was probably too late in most cases. Still, it was worth a try; I couldn't work at Harry's forever.

The following day at the betting shop, most of the conversation revolved around Wellington Day. The front page of the *Sporting Life* actually carried a summary of the race, and the writer concluded that Wellington Day looked a good thing for Cheltenham, and perhaps a contender for the Champion Hurdle the following year.

'I'll bet Michael's pleased with this,' I said, pointing out the article to Harry.

'He should be, it was one hell of a race.'

I spent most of the day on automatic pilot, just making sure Arthur got the right results for the right races and the correct odds down during the shows of betting. But my mind was on the events of the last couple of months.

I had posted eight of the application forms on my way into work, and it was now a question of sitting back and waiting for the interviews, if any materialised. But I couldn't help thinking how different it would all be if I had Katie. I was still miserable, but that was only to be expected.

By mid-afternoon I was getting bored. It was very quiet in the shop so I asked Harry if he minded if I went early. I hadn't got anything particular to do, but I felt the need to go somewhere lively. I wanted to be amongst people who had things happening to them.

I caught a tube to Piccadilly Circus and stood against a lamppost, just watching the buzz of people around me and the lights of the various advertisements changing. Automatically I reached into my pocket for my cigarettes. There was only one left in the packet so I decided this would definitely be the last. It was then I realised that I was actually standing outside quite a large chemist's shop, so with a very deliberate act of defiance against my weakness I threw the empty packet and the one remaining cigarette into a wastepaper bin.

I marched into the shop and up to the counter next to the prescriptions, and looked expectantly at a middle-aged lady who had just finished serving.

'Can I help you?' she asked.

'I hope so. I want some gum to stop me from smoking.'

'Yes, sir, there are a number of things on the market.'

'No, I want a particular type.'

'What is it called?' was her natural reply.

'Ah well, there's the problem; I don't know. But you can't possibly miss it, in fact if you'd seen it you'd never forget it, because it's wrapped in this bright . . .' I paused and my voice began to falter, '. . . this bright . . . green . . . green . . .' I suddenly felt ill. My head started to spin. 'Of course . . . of course, that's the answer!' I said aloud. Somewhere in the distance I could hear the assistant asking if I was all right, but by then I was walking quickly towards the exit, my mind in a state of shock.

I really couldn't believe it, but it had to be the answer to the Davidson question and the letters.

I found a phone box and made two calls, the first to Frankie Allen. Then I went back into the underground and caught a tube to Euston. There I bought a ticket and got on the train.

My mind was a blur for most the journey. Surely it wasn't possible, and yet I had to be right – it was the only answer. The fact that I had been granted an audience for that evening really confirmed it.

It must have been about eight o'clock when I got off the train and began to walk into the familiar city centre. The shops were all closed for the night and there were very few pedestrians around. I found my way easily to the office building. I had been told on the telephone that the staff entrance to the side would be left open for me, and sure enough it was.

I climbed the dark staircase very cautiously, but when I reached the corridor the light from the office shining through the half-open door made my direction easier.

I didn't bother knocking, I just walked straight in, and for a second the two occupants of the room were startled.

'Good evening, Mr Davidson,' I said, to set the scene.

He didn't bat an eyelid, just stared at me with those same cold, evil eyes. 'Well, it was as good a name as any.'

'I suppose so. Had you signed the letters George Ellerton, I wouldn't have taken any notice.'

I had only been in Ellerton's office once before – the day he'd told me I was going to be the advertising sales rep for the newspaper. I remembered that day clearly: Ellerton had not invited me to sit down then, and this day was no different, except this time I felt more comfortable standing.

Ellerton was perched behind his enormous antique oak desk, looking like some termite that had just crawled out of the woodwork. His angular, gaunt face was just as I remembered it, but the greying hair was now more salt than pepper. He still had that same expression of hate fixed on his face, the one I remembered when I woke up in the hospital and found him looking down at me.

The other man in the room I vaguely recognised, but couldn't place. He stood uneasily to my left by the window, watching Ellerton as if controlled by his reflexes.

As I glanced back at Ellerton, his top lip lifted in a sneer at one corner. 'You really are a clever little bastard,' he said. 'How ever did you make the connection between me and the letters?'

'Would you believe it was Frankie Allen's chewing gum?' I answered, quite pleased with myself.

'What are you talking about?' The irritation was already starting to show in his voice.

'Well, for some reason you must know Frankie Allen,' I said, looking for confirmation.

'We've done business together . . . and although Allen doesn't want to, we're going to be doing some more.' It came across more as a threat than a statement. I could never imagine anybody threatening Frankie Allen, but then maybe Allen and Ellerton were in the same league, at least as far as local muscle went. Regardless, that was obviously the impression he was trying to sell me.

'You see,' I continued, 'Frankie Allen had to be the key. He was the one with all the information on the horses, and then I connected him to you through the chewing gum.' I was beginning to feel like the prosecution in a criminal court and, knowing I'd got the case stitched up, I was actually starting to enjoy the situation. 'You see, Allen has this special chewing gum to stop him smoking. It's wrapped in an unmistakable bright green paper and this particular gum is exceptionally difficult to get hold of. I was trying to describe it in a chemist's shop when I suddenly realised where I had seen the paper before. Last November I happened to bump into your wife, purely by accident,' I tried to make it sound insignificant for fear of any reprisal, 'at Wolverhampton races, and she gave me a lift back to the station in your Mercedes. The ashtray on the passenger side was stuffed full of bright green wrapping paper. It just had to be Frankie Allen who put it there, so before I phoned you this afternoon I rang him and asked if he knew you. Having discovered that he did, the whole story pieced together.' Then I asked Ellerton the question to which I already knew the answer. 'The whole thing was all aimed at me, wasn't it? There was no coup, just a vendetta.'

'No, of course there was no coup. In fact the whole thing was Buckley's idea.' He gestured towards the other man in the room. 'Not knowing anything about horse-racing, I didn't think it would work; I couldn't believe you would be so stupid or gullible. But then gamblers all appear to have that same mentality, like lemmings . . . and you certainly jumped off the cliff with the rest of them.' It was his turn to look smug and self-satisfied, but there was more to it than that; that evil undercurrent was still there, and the accused obviously still thought he was calling the shots. 'I'll fill in the details,' he continued with a sneered smile, 'because it won't make any difference now.'

For the first time since entering the room I began to feel uneasy.

'You probably know that I prevented you from getting employment in the Midlands, but when you went to London I knew it would be much harder to make life difficult for you, so I employed Buckley here,' again he gestured towards the other man, 'to keep an eye on you. You see, he's a private investigator, or at least he was, but I don't think they give licences, or whatever they issue private eyes with, to people who get done for grievous bodily harm. Anyway, Buckley followed you for quite some time, then when he told me about your tatty little job in that bookmaker's my first inclination was to get you kicked out, but I thought that might not be quite so easy.'

He went on to tell me it was about the same time as he first went into association with Frankie Allen, and Buckley, who knew about Allen's tipping business, had suggested the letters.

The idea was simple: send tips indirectly to me via Arthur, that way I wouldn't suspect anything, then build me up to the extent where I would be so convinced the final horse would win that I would hopefully put all I owned and more on it, and of course the horse would lose.

It was just a game to Ellerton, a minor bit of amusement until he could come up with something better.

'But of course it didn't work,' I said. 'Brass Lock, the supposed failure, actually won.'

'Yes, it did. You must have won a fucking fortune – well, at least in your paltry terms,' his disparaging tone continued.

'I wouldn't call it a fortune, but it was very nice all the same,' I said sarcastically.

'Apart from that last horse winning, the scheme actually worked. And

I even tried to cater for Brass Lock winning. I got Buckley and a friend of his to follow you the day of the race, just in case by some mishap you won. The idea was to relieve you of the cash, but Buckley cocked it up, didn't you, Buckley?'

'We could have got you on the train,' Buckley volunteered, 'except that crowd of kids jumped on.'

Of course, that's where I had seen him before – the two men on the train! I hadn't liked the look of him then and he looked worse in close-up. Still, since Ellerton wasn't yet pulling the cords to work him, I turned my attention from the puppet back to the master. I was confused about Frankie Allen's involvement, so I asked Ellerton how he got the tips.

'Oh, getting the information was easy. I just asked Allen if he could pass on a few winners to me. He really didn't take much notice himself, just gave me the name of the man who handled that side of the business and told him to co-operate. He was extremely helpful; each time I phoned he would tell me how good the tip was. Told me Towerstack was a fucking certainty. Just shows what a mug's game it is.'

'Tell me what happened to Mrs Clifford,' I said solemnly.

Buckley looked nervous, but Ellerton pulled a string. 'Go on, tell him, it doesn't matter now.'

'Well, after it all went wrong,' Buckley started nervously, 'Mr Ellerton worried that something might implicate him, so to be on the safe side he sent me to check the old man's flat and get the letters back, if he still had them. I waited outside for the right moment, so when they went out that Sunday lunchtime I got into the flat . . .'

'How did you get in?' I interrupted.

'Easy. I've got keys that fit most locks. Anyway, I got in and started looking around. I'd just found the letters in the kitchen when the stupid old woman came back. The cow tried to grab them off me; I just shoved her out of the way and she fell against the cooker.'

'You callous bastard,' I said, anger welling up inside. 'Why didn't you take the money on the television?'

'Mr Ellerton said I wasn't to make it look like a break-in, and after the old woman fell I got out as quickly as I could.'

I turned to Ellerton. 'So he's guilty . . .' it was my turn to gesture towards Buckley, '. . . at least of manslaughter, I guess. And I don't know what that puts you down for.'

'I suppose you must feel quite pleased with yourself,' Ellerton said. 'Solved a mystery and identified a killer.'

And I did feel pleased with myself, but I was also becoming extremely concerned. For a condemned man, Ellerton was taking it all far too well. My intention had been to go in and confront him as I had done, then hand everything I knew over to the police. But now Ellerton was sitting at his desk, smiling all over his face. Had I made a miscalculation somewhere?

'The fact is, Simms, you've solved a little problem for me too. You see, after the car accident with you and Elaine, I've never really trusted her, so when I went to the States I told Buckley to keep an eye on her. And surprise, surprise! Who does she spend the night with but her old lover. Before, I could never be totally sure there was anything between you, but there was my concrete evidence. When Buckley told me, I decided I would have to kill you.'

That was the moment I should have made a run for it, but I didn't. A second later it was too late, because he opened a drawer in his desk and took out a gun.

At first I thought he was just trying to frighten me, and if that was the case then he was doing a bloody good job. I wondered if I should tell him so. But there was a wild look in his eyes and instinct told me he was serious.

'Don't be insane, Ellerton,' I said. 'You'd never get away with it.' It must have sounded like a line out of a poor 'B' movie, but under the circumstances it was the best I could do.

'Why not?' he asked, as he rose from his chair and walked around to the front of the desk. 'Well-respected Midlands businessman is working late in his office one evening, when a man he sacked twelve months ago breaks in for revenge. I would have to shoot you in self-defence.' He turned to the puppet. 'You've got a gun he can have, haven't you, Buckley?'

Buckley tapped his pocket and nodded in a movement that was synchronised perfection.

'But we won't give it to him until he's dead, will we?' Ellerton said with obvious amusement. He was now leaning back against the desk. His hand was shaking slightly but the gun was still pointed at me, as it had been since he had taken it out of the drawer.

I wondered how far from the door I was; it was a big office and I wasn't sure just how far in I'd come. I thought I'd left it half open, but I didn't dare take my eyes off my ex-employer. His eyes had glazed over and his whole face had taken on a kind of crazed look. I'd always suspected him to be bordering on the insane, but now I was convinced. Story of my life – I wise up too late!

'Nobody takes anything I own and gets away with it, Simms. Do you understand that now?' If my head had been attached to a string I would have nodded, but then I don't suppose it would have made much difference. He lifted the gun up to eye level, like a child taking aim.

My mind was telling me to run, but my feet seemed super-glued to the spot. On the television I had often watched people being shot, but it had never occurred to me what it would be like to be on the receiving end of a bullet. Suddenly I found myself wondering: would it be painful? Would I ever know anything about it?

Why waste time wondering? I was about to find out. His finger moved on the trigger and the explosion echoed around the room. I staggered back a couple of feet, my brain searching my body for pain – but I could find nothing. He'd missed; I was convinced he'd missed. I was about to burn the rubber off the bottom of my shoes when I noticed Ellerton. The crazed expression was still on his face, but it was cemented on and he was starting to slide slowly down the desk, a carnation of red creeping out over his white shirt.

I looked across at Buckley, but he was as surprised as I was.

'Both of you stand exactly where you are.' The voice came from behind me and I turned to see Frankie Allen standing by the door, a gun in his right hand pointing in the general direction of me and Buckley. He moved swiftly over to Ellerton's body. I noticed he was as immaculately dressed as ever, except this time he was also wearing a pair of tight black gloves.

He switched his gun into his left hand and carefully took Ellerton's weapon from his lifeless fingers. 'You. Move towards the door.' I was just about to do as he said, when I realised he was motioning towards Buckley, not me.

Buckley seemed lost without someone to operate the controls. He hesitated, but then did as he was told. Just as he got to the door Allen fired without warning and two shots thudded deafeningly into Buckley's body, sending him reeling back against the wall.

I tried to say something but my mouth wouldn't work. I just stared at the horrifying scene – two corpses sprawled out on the floor.

Allen carefully placed Ellerton's gun back in his hand, and then went over to the other body and forced the gun he had used to shoot Ellerton into Buckley's hand.

'Have you touched anything?' he said, his voice without the slightest trace of emotion.

I managed to shake my head.

'Right then, be careful on your way out.'

'He's … he's …' my voice came out as a croak, '… got a gun in … in his pocket.' I pointed to Buckley.

Allen was quickly down and fished the gun out of the dead man's jacket. He looked up. 'Well done, I think you're getting the hang of this.' Then he grabbed me by the arm, dragged me down the corridor and out into the street.

'I touched the door handle,' I said.

'I wiped it on the way in,' was his almost incidental reply.

Wolverhampton was usually quiet on Monday nights, and sure enough the street was deserted. Allen told me to walk beside him and look as natural as possible so as not to draw attention to ourselves. We walked for about five minutes and then he stopped by a fairly inconspicuous car, opened the door and guided me into the passenger seat. He went around to the driver's side and shut the door. 'I'll drive you to Birmingham station.' He waited for some response but I was too dazed to answer. 'You did come by train?'

I nodded.

'From there you get a train to London and a tube home. No taxis, no going to the bar on the train, nothing at all that might get you noticed. Got it?' He was speaking like a teacher to a child and, feeling like a delinquent, I nodded again to indicate I understood.

The car headed in the direction of Birmingham and for the second time that evening I said, 'You'll never get away with it.'

'Why not? Buckley had a string of violent offences against him and Ellerton, what was it he said to you, he would shoot in self-defence?'

'How do you know what he said to me?' I asked, surprised.

'Because I arrived there at the same time as you, so I just followed you in but stayed out of sight.'

'But why were you there at all?'

'When you phoned and asked if I knew Ellerton, I realised what was going on. Do you remember the first time you came to my office and I said I thought I recognised you? Well, it wasn't you I recognised, it was your name, but it didn't register until you mentioned Ellerton. You see, the first time I met Ellerton he was ranting on about somebody called Simms, saying he was going to get even with him for screwing his wife. He also asked for some tips on the horses; at that time I did-n't take any notice, we were going to do a little business together, so if he wanted tips he could have them. When you phoned and asked if I knew him, I put two and two together.'

'Did you think he was going to kill me?' I asked.

'I had no idea, but his actions didn't surprise me. Ellerton was deranged; my mistake was getting involved with him. At first we worked together on a few nice little deals of mutual benefit. But then he start-ed to get greedy; he came up with some hare-brained scheme which needed the help of my organisation. I told him I wasn't interested and that's when he started trying to put the pressure on. He actually tried blackmail to make me collaborate with him. Now I couldn't have that, could I? He just had to go. So don't flatter yourself, Simms; I'm no knight in shining armour coming to your rescue. I just took the situation as it stood and turned it to my advantage.'

'I'm glad you did,' I said, although in all honesty I wasn't sure that I was. 'Why are we going to Birmingham?'

'Because Birmingham station is much busier than Wolverhampton and there's less chance of you being noticed. I always work on the assumption that if you don't leave loose ends you don't get tied up.'

'But won't the police be out now looking for us or something?'

'Why ever should they? I'd think it unlikely the bodies will be found until tomorrow.'

'But the shots?'

'They might have sounded loud in the room, but outside anybody hearing them would probably assume it was just a car backfiring. After all, people in Wolverhampton are not exactly used to hearing gunfire. Don't worry about it, just keep a low profile and keep away from Ellerton's missus.' Of that he was emphatic.

He dropped me at Birmingham New Street Station and I bought a ticket for London.

I sat down in the brightly lit carriage and stared out of the window into darkness. It was then that the enormity of the situation closed in on me. Because of my affair with Elaine Ellerton, three people were now dead: Ellerton, Buckley and, worst of all, Arthur's wife. I started to shake uncontrollably. Keep a low profile . . . Keep a low profile . . . I tried.

9

I awoke with a start and sat bolt upright in bed. I wasn't sure where I was, but someone was knocking on the window.

Very slowly reality dawned like a bad dream, and I let my head fall gently back onto the pillow. Nobody could be knocking on the window, at least not without a very long ladder.

I lay in bed listening to the rain hammering relentlessly against the glass. The room was cold, but then it always was. My head ached and my mouth felt dry from constant drinking. Over the last five or six weeks I had become used to waking up that way.

My mind drifted back to my birthday, the day when it all started: Katie, the tips, everything. Basically, nothing much had changed for me; I was still living in a dump of a bedsitter and still working for H. Greenaway Turf Accountant, at least when I could drag myself in. The only differences were that now I had some money, Katie had gone, and three people were dead.

After the horrific episode with Ellerton and Frankie Allen, I had returned to my flat and virtually stayed there in a drunken stupor for about a week. On the days when I could get up, I would walk down to the corner shop for the papers, just to be ready when the police came calling. But no connection had been made, either with me or Frankie Allen. At first the story attracted significant media coverage, but the conclusions drawn by the press and police alike were those predicted by Allen.

Nevertheless, the thought of three killings, coupled with my loss of Katie, seemed to be more than I could stand. After my initial drunken blitz, Jim's wife had dragged me off to the doctor, who diagnosed depression and prescribed tablets of some kind or other. They didn't make me any better, they just put me into a duped state of oblivion – I didn't care what happened to me.

I struggled out of bed feeling lousy. The tablets weren't meant for headaches but I took three anyway. I got dressed, but couldn't even be bothered to make a cup of coffee.

I picked up a cassette and looked at the face of Karen Carpenter smiling up from the cover. The late Karen Carpenter; I wondered if she was happy at last, but I didn't even put the cassette on – must have been the tablets starting to work.

I dressed and walked to the door, briefly stopping to look at the new pile of unopened letters sitting on the sideboard. Collecting unopened mail was getting to be a habit.

As I walked downstairs, sure enough a neatly typed envelope addressed to Mr D. Simms was sitting on the table. Most days I'd left the mail until I returned, but somehow this one lying alone on the table brought back memories of my birthday, and almost absent-mindedly I put it in my inside pocket.

It was raining outside, but generally the weather seemed to be getting slightly warmer. I had intended to go to work, but walking through the rain seemed to bring Katie back to the forefront of my thoughts, so I just kept walking and talking to her in my mind.

After a few hours of aimless walking, I found myself on the embankment. I sauntered slowly along, my thoughts on the events of the last four months, until eventually I found myself at St Paul's. I looked up, my memory jumping through clouds, like the ones which seemed so close to the giant cross on the top of the building. I went up the first steps into the cathedral and started the long climb up the stairs. When I could get no higher, I stepped through the small door and out into the wind and lashing rain.

Not surprisingly I was the only person up there. I stood pressed against the wall looking at the Thames winding away into forever. Katie seemed to be there with me, and in my mind I heard her telling me to go to the railing to get a better view. 'Don't be silly,' she teased, 'you can't fall off . . . not unless you actually climb it . . .'

I moved hesitantly towards the rails which came up to my chest, and then I stepped onto the horizontal bar about six inches off the floor. From there I started to lean into nowhere.

Something was pressing under my arm. It was the envelope. Instantly another vision of the past came flooding back: Katie laughing as I whipped out my birthday card, 'just like James Bond going for his gun.'

Still standing on the rail, I took out the envelope. There was a card inside. A card? But it wasn't my birthday. The day? What day? My mind fought to remember: Monday 14 February – Valentine's Day.

I pulled the card from the envelope and opened it. There was nothing written inside, but then I smiled and started to laugh. On the inside cover were two Co-op stamps.